THIS WAS MR B

DAVID PATTISON

A WOTLARX ENTERPRISE

THIS WAS MR BLEANEY'S BIKE

Published by
Wotlarx Enterprises
1007 Anlaby High Road
Hull Yorkshire HU4 7PN
England

Enquiries to wotlarx-books@hotmail.co.uk

Cover design by Jane Anderson (www.janeanderson.co.uk)

ISBN 0-9554130-0-1
ISBN 978-9554130-0-1

Also by David Pattison

Poetry
Casting a Faint Shadow
The Face on the Page
At the Firefly Café (due Spring 2007)

Non-Fiction
No Room for Cowardice

Plays
The List
Tribunal
Boots

For Polly

ONE

An unusual inheritance

On his death five years ago Albert Bleaney, 'enigmatic poet of the working class' (the *Guardian*), left his house and contents to Molly Ripley, the woman who had shared his last years. Apart from bequeathing the royalties 'from the works published at the time of my death to the Society of Authors', which led to mild speculation that some unpublished works might exist, the only other bequest was made to Sludge who inherited his friend's bicycle. It was handed over to him at a bizarre ceremony when, clearly following the terms of the will, an embarrassed solicitor pushed an ancient and battered Raleigh Roadster in Sludge's direction with the words, 'This was Mr Bleaney's bike.'

In her turn and after some years of alcohol-induced confusion Molly died and left the house and its contents (largely untouched since Albert's death) to the Albert Bleaney Society, which was formed on the poet's death, 'to preserve his memory and promote his works'. The 200 plus members received newsletters twice a year and were invited to the occasional discussion group. This year an inaugural walk, led by Ronan Coyne, a sometime rambler and university lecturer from Leeds whose fervency was considered deeply suspect by Sludge, was to take place in and around Ottingham, a small featureless village just two or three miles from the University. The untidy collection of houses and shops was once situated in open countryside, but had been almost completely swallowed up by the encroaching suburbs of Kingston. Here Albert Bleaney was born and went to school. The walk was to take place in eight days time on the Saturday of the coming week.

Some weeks after Molly's funeral when the niceties had been settled in a long enough time to justify the solicitor's extortionate bill, Sludge and Pamela were standing in the book lined living room cum study of 105 West Bank. The society now had possession of the house and contents and the pair had agreed to carry out a preliminary inspection, and to report back to the Committee the following day.

The first and only house owned by the poet was a smallish rather uncomfortable detached house to the west of the city centre in an area struggling to hold the status once given to it by the presence of trawler skippers and their glamorous wives with their beehive hair, but who had drifted away when the fishing industry collapsed. Now populated by retired executives wearing paisley cravats and deck shoes and beige clad spinsters living out their days of faded gentility it was, thought Sludge, an appropriate place for a dead poet's society to settle.

Something is found, and a decision is made

Holding a small square transparent envelope to the window Sludge squinted at the contents: half a dozen small pink oval shapes of a thin and delicate substance, and a small tight curl of what appeared to be honey coloured threads. 'This is a most peculiar sort of bookmark. These are flower petals,' he indicated the pink shapes, 'knowing Albert's love of D H Lawrence some sort of daisy I should think. The other' he smiled at his companion Pamela Paynter who had found the envelope between the pages of *The Collected Poems of Thomas Hardy*, 'is definitely pubic hair.'

Glancing through the window while Pamela digested this news he considered how this revelation might complicate the decision he had made earlier that day to murder Dr Peter Pelham, a fellow lecturer at the University of the East Riding, known privately to Sludge as Poisonous Pete because, according to Sludge, he poisoned everything around him.

He had decided to kill Pelham as the result of an expression he had seen flicker across his colleague's face at the staff meeting that morning. It was only the briefest of glances that he caught, but it was enough to convince him that murder was the only solution.

He had seen that look before. It was in the 1950s black and white film *Attack* starring Jack Palance and Eddie Albert. GI sergeant Jack Palance had been run over by a tank and, reasonably enough, was dying. But before he died he had something to do. He had to kill Eddie Albert. Half-falling, half-crawling, dragging his broken body down the steps of the underground bunker that had been their headquarters Jack raised a bloody hand skyward and pleaded, 'God, give me one more minute. Just one more minute'. In the bunker Eddie Albert, the craven army captain whose cowardice had sent his men to certain death, whimpered as he listened to Jack's approach. God didn't give Jack the extra minute he needed and he died on the steps, falling into the bunker at Eddie's feet. Terror stricken Eddie looked at Jack, but as he realised that his would-be nemesis was dead a change came over him. He straightened up, his shoulders went back, he clenched and unclenched his fists. Tilting his head, he looked upwards and sideways. The fear left his eyes and a strange and secret smile slowly spread itself across his face. That was the look Sludge had seen before. A look that said, 'I've got away with it. No one can touch me now.'

Unobtrusively Sludge looked around at his colleagues, trying to determine whether anyone else realised what had just happened. There were fifteen of them sitting at a long table in a room that was high and wide. At one end of the room a huge mahogany fireplace and overmantel dominated. Still known as the Senior Common Room (in a previous existence it had been just that) the room now served as a general meeting place for University staff. As usual with Faculty meetings, the only point of agreement was destined to be the date of the next meeting, and that only after lengthy discussion. Sludge was bitterly disappointed that the 'issues' around Pelham's behaviour had been fudged. He'd seen the look on his adversary's face; Pelham knew he had escaped again. It was worse than that. Sludge knew that it would be a long time, if ever, before 'these matters' could be reconsidered.

Dr Peter Edgar Pelham was the only member of staff in the department who taught Business Studies. A qualified plumbing engineer now specialising in Organisational Behaviour, Pelham used the rigid logic of his former profession in transforming the 'touchy feely' approach to behavioural studies to one where two and two always made four and water could only ever be either hot or cold. Apart from this notable achievement he was also, according to Sludge, probably the only member of staff who was a rapist and a murderer.

Almost exactly two years ago on a cool evening in May a Japanese girl had fallen from the roof of the Library. After a short investigation the coroner's inquest recorded a verdict of suicide. At the request of the family the fact that she was pregnant had not been made public. As the

4

last person known to have spoken to the girl before she died Pelham gave evidence at the inquest. He said that the girl had been worried about her marks, and he cried when he said that he thought he had managed to convince her that 'she was O.K'. Subsequent rumours about Pelham's involvement with the girl were unsubstantiated and quickly squashed by the University.

It was quite sometime later that Sludge heard unusable but very reliable evidence that his fellow lecturer was offering to change poor marks for good marks to female students in exchange for 'certain favours'. It was rumoured that Pelham was responsible for the Japanese girl's pregnancy. It was also rumoured that she had an appointment with the Dean to whom she was going to tell all. Sludge had been able to find out that the girl had arranged an appointment with the Dean. It was for ten o'clock in the morning of the day following her death.

All this information, which effectively proved nothing, was harmful to Sludge. Such knowledge only served to emphasise his impotence. He had organised a desultory whispering campaign that had come to nothing and his latest objections - to Pelham's nomination for the vacant post of Department Head, a position he was more interested in than he could admit, even to himself - were received with scorn. The Dean of the Faculty, Desiree Croucher, a large lady whose once merely mediocre looks had now faded into a quite spectacular ugliness, had been particularly dismissive. A woman of fascinating personal habits the Dean was much given to dramatic statements that she emphasised by placing the back of a crooked wrist beneath one of her massive breasts and heaving it to one side while turning her head in the opposite direction and sniffing in peremptory fashion. Dean Croucher, with much breast heaving and sniffing, had told Sludge unequivocally that Pelham was a very valued member of staff and that Sludge's constant sniping was ill-judged and undermining any ambitions or pretensions he might have had for higher office within the University. In short, he had been told to shut up and get on with his job. This was, he was reminded, to approve the progress of as many students as possible. In this respect he had been advised to seek counsel from Peter Pelham who had an excellent record for getting students through to successful completion of his courses. Sludge's bitter response, that she 'define success for me', had been pointedly ignored.

It would be reasonable to assume that Sludge was distressed by the way the meeting had gone. The 'lamentable events' of two years ago had been consigned to history and any faint hopes of resurrecting an internal inquiry had gone with them. In addition, Sludge's vague hopes for personal advancement had been severely jolted. However, as he walked across the campus, nodding to students here and there, he was angry, but he was also very relaxed. He had made a decision to resolve his problems once and for all. If the University wouldn't act, then he would. He had decided to kill Pelham. All he needed now was a plan.

Sludge considered why he was prepared to kill his adversary. Even if he wasn't a murderer and a rapist he was still a dangerous lying and manipulative unprincipled bastard, he thought. A man who cheated both students and the university as a matter of routine and made Sludge look so foolish and unworldly as to be unpromotable. A man who enjoyed the decline in educative standards because it allowed him to adopt a superior 'we had it tough in my day' stance. A man who snorted rather than laughed, chewed his fingernails and spat out the pieces, and a man who wore a large silver ring with a black stone on which his initials, PEP, were engraved in silver. Was this enough to kill him?

Probably not, thought Sludge, but he was fully aware that the making of the plan would be enough to ease his feelings of hatred for Poisonous Pete. If he could pretend to himself that he was going to remove the cause of some of his personal difficulties then that might ease his mind long enough for him to come up with a less drastic course of action. On the other hand, there was no denying that his life would be so much more enjoyable if the poisonous one was removed.

Dr William S Ludgeworth

Pamela Paynter had moved to Kingston three years ago with her husband who had taken a post as Headmaster of Thomas Stratten Sixth Form College and had immediately joined the Albert Bleaney Society. The Membership Secretary, Joan Sanderson, on learning that she was a qualified accountant promptly asked her to become the treasurer. Pamela accepted the honour and was happy to play a full part in the Society's activities. Of the other committee members, Beryl Crockford and Joan she found to be 'absolutely charming', Ronan Coyne she considered an 'odious self-serving little man' and Sludge was almost a closed book, to her, and to most others she admitted to herself.

She looked at Sludge's back as he stood at the window, and not for the first time, wondered why he had stayed in this pleasant but small backwater town. She knew a little about him: that he was Dr William S Ludgeworth, known to his students (and many others) as Billy Sludge. Of medium build with close-cropped hair and a liking for black drape jackets, he was known as a man of idiosyncratic style. She knew that he was not much given to the company of others and would have described him as self sufficient and self contained, a solitary man rather than a lonely one. A former partner, Sheila, who had also taught at the University, was somewhere in the background. She had heard stories that the couple had simply agreed to go different ways for a trial period that had now extended to several years.

Dr William S Ludgeworth (Sheila took his name for Sludgeworth and coined the nickname Billy Sludge) was a senior lecturer in the School of Arts and Humanities at the University of the East Riding on the north east coast of England where his speciality subject was African Literature. He had once been tipped as an academic high flyer but things hadn't turned out that way. A Bachelor of Arts degree (with first class honours) from a 'good' university followed by a doctorate and a well-received critical textbook before he was twenty-six was his passport to a lucrative two year post at the University of Texas. The University supported his application for a non-immigrant visa with the promise that they would endorse his eventual application for a Green Card that would allow him to take up permanent employment in the United States.

Unfortunately his involvement in campus politics and his enthusiastic support of student led protest movements aimed at the policies of President Ronald Reagan, resulted in the abrupt cancellation of his contract by the University and the withdrawal of his visa by the State Department. A photograph, which had appeared on the front page of the Dallas Morning News, showing Sludge in the vanguard of a phalanx of students facing the guns of the National Guard, was produced as evidence of his unsuitability when he asked for the withdrawal to be reconsidered. Several students had been injured in that incident, some of them very seriously, when the Guard charged the line and used rifle butts indiscriminately and with devastating effect. Sludge's departure, even though it was not of his own volition, left him feeling that somehow he had failed them. Although he considered it to be of secondary importance, he was also aware that by losing his job in such circumstances he had taken a large backward step, in what so far had been a painless and untrammelled road to academic success and renown. There were plusses: he had gained respect and a liking for students he had never felt when he was a student himself. He had also discovered, to his cost, the expedient and nakedly political nature of the decision making process in large institutions. However, how one could remain true to the former while playing the games demanded by the latter was a dilemma he couldn't resolve.

When he arrived at Houston International Airport for his flight to London he was greeted at the check-in desk by a humourless man wearing mirror shades who delivered the advice that as far as the United States of America was concerned he was declared *persona non grata*. 'In short, Chief' the official had said 'don't try to come back. We have enough crazy people of our own, we don't need to import them.' The six hours he had to wait in Chicago for a connecting flight was spent isolated with an anonymous official who spoke only to confirm the same uncompromising message.

Issues of academic success and renown were a long way from his mind on his return to England. Blacklisted by the Americans and without a reference from his employer, he had taken a post in what he knew was an academic backwater, but one that would satisfy his need for a bolthole while he recovered from the trauma of his Texas experience. The University of the East Riding did have at least one attraction in that it was less than a two-hour drive north to his hometown, where his brother and his parents still lived. Seventeen years later, he was still there.

Sludge was aware that those seventeen years had more or less drifted by. Perhaps, he thought, he had been traumatised by the American experience, or more prosaically; he was quite simply not cut out to be in the vanguard of anything. Whatever the reason he was determined that he should now try to influence circumstances rather than the other way round. If he could have added the ability to see into the future to his new found decisiveness, Sludge would have been able to see that he was about to become involved in a series of incredible events that would change his life for ever.

Pamela Paynter, who knew very little of Sludge's history, thought one of the reasons he appeared to have settled in the area, apart from a seemingly obvious lack of ambition, was the friendship he had formed with the locally based, somewhat reclusive poet Albert Bleaney, who, perhaps among other things, shared Sludge's liking for drinking stout and listening to the music of Bob Dylan.

If, in her turn, Pamela had been blessed with the seer's eye then she would have known that Sludge's American experience and his friendship with the poet were about to become linked in the most remarkable fashion.

TWO

The famous four

'Pubic hair? Really?' she said 'Does it say whose it is?' A lover of Thomas Hardy's poetry Pamela had taken the volume from one of the shelves and immediately noticed the plastic envelope when the book fell open. It had a small metal clip attached to the back that suggested it might once have held a name badge or something similar. Appropriately enough it appeared to be marking the poem, 'On a Discovered Curl of Hair'.

'Yes, it is definitely pubic hair.' Sludge replied 'No name, but as it is blond that eliminates the famous four.'

The 'famous four' were four women Albert Bleaney had met in his early life, had fallen in love with and because, as he said 'I never learned how to fall out of love' had regarded them as his constant companions. Joan Sanderson and Beryl Crockford he had known since Grammar School days, June Kingston had been at his first poetry reading in 1952 when the poet was 20 years old and Molly Ripley met him three years later when she was working as an assistant in a city centre bookshop. All four had lived with Albert Bleaney on and off, at various times over the years. Joan and Beryl were the joint driving forces behind the formation of the Albert Bleaney Society. It was only after careful thought that Sludge had accepted their invitation to join them as founding committee members although June had for 'personal reasons' graciously declined the same invitation and Molly simply failed to respond. Pamela and Ronan Coyne, who was only elected after he had lobbied very hard, made up the rest of the committee.

It was, or so Joan, Beryl and June claimed, merely Molly's good luck that she was in residence when the poet died. Inspection of his last will and testament tended to support that view. It appeared that the will had been drawn up leaving all his property to, 'My companion at the time of my death..........' Two days before his death he had written in Molly's name, signed and dated the insertion. The alteration was signed and witnessed by William S Ludgeworth.

Not unreasonably each of the others argued that if they had been in favour at that time they would have inherited everything. After Albert's death Molly became reclusive, began to drink heavily and allowed the other three, who remained tolerably good friends, only very occasional access to Albert's former home. The surviving three had in fact attended Molly's funeral, had seen her interred in a plot some twenty metres from the poet's grave. This was an opportunity too good to miss for the local paper which carried a photograph of the black clad trio leaving the church under the banner headline 'Leaving the Church', which was clearly a reference to Bleaney's poem celebrating the demise of organised religion.

So who's 'caverned ark' had Albert visited.' said Sludge reading from the Thomas Hardy poem 'It must have been a very special occasion' he added, half to himself. 'Just a minute' he looked closely at the small envelope 'something has been written here, some numbers by the look of it. It has faded badly but whoever wrote it had to press very hard and the marks are still there. It looks like a date.' Turning his back to the window so that the light came over his shoulder he peered at the envelope. 'Yes, it seems to be a date; I can just make it out, seventeen, seven, eighty-five.' he read out the numbers slowly, 'The seventeenth of July 1985. Now that rings a bell. Why should it? Does it mean anything to you, Pamela?'

Pamela shook her head, 'Perhaps the diaries will help.' she said, 'If they exist.' she added with a smile.

'Oh, yes, they exist,' said Sludge 'they certainly exist'.

Sludge turned back to the window. There was more to the mystery of the diaries than Pamela knew. Shortly after Albert's death Molly had been visited by a stranger she described as 'a clean-cut military type, very persuasive, but cold with it' who had asked if he could buy anything unusual connected with the poet. He had also asked if he could look at any diaries or records Albert had left. Sludge knew that the stranger, or perhaps different strangers, had turned up at regular intervals over the years, always asking the same questions about 'anything unusual' and about the diaries. Molly, who had told Sludge that she had never seen the diaries had also confided that she felt the house had been searched on several occasions but he had put that down to whisky induced paranoia. What Sludge also knew was that similar types, Albert called them 'my very own SAS men', had called on him several times over the last years of his life. He refused to elaborate, instead he laughed and said 'National security, old cock but my diaries will tell all, never failing to add to this by 'singing' in a Dylanesque growl 'The man in the trench coat / Badge out, laid off / Says he's got a bad cough / Wants to get it paid off / Look out kid / It's something I did.' Of course Sludge had recognised the lines from *Subterranean Homesick Blues*, and although he had listened to the lyrics many times, apart from spotting that the last line quoted by Albert Bleaney should have been 'It's something you did' rather than 'Something I did', he had failed to find anything that pointed to the whereabouts of the diaries.

Looking gloomily at the weeds growing through the cracked concrete driveway and then at the rain clouds drifting slowly overhead, 'Oh yes' he murmured, 'the diaries exist. But where the hell are they?'

Fabio Brindisi

Apart from his friendship with Albert Bleaney, another benefit of his long stay in the 'northern fishing town' (a disgruntled local had once told Sludge that although his home town had suffered more damage from the Luftwaffe in World War Two than either Coventry or London it was a little known fact, because for 'strategic reasons' the town was never named, but only ever referred to in the newspapers and on the radio as a 'northern fishing town'), perhaps the only other benefit, he was ready to concede, was that he had eventually managed to acquire one of the most comfortable rooms on the campus.

Three buildings - rather grandly called halls, built in the 1920s and each named after local heroes, Carter, Moore and Burbanks - were placed around the curved side of a semi-circular lawn, the straight edge of which ran parallel with the tree-lined avenue giving access to the campus. Beyond the halls with their stone-mullioned windows and ivy-clad walls, was a motley collection of buildings providing seminar and lecture rooms, an administration block and some student accommodation. Erected over the years as funds became available, these various buildings, some built of glass, others in grey pre-cast concrete slabs and others using traditional red brick, were in themselves a condemnation of a series of builders and architects who had steadfastly refused to be anything other than contemporary.

Sludge had a room on the third (top) floor in Carter looking down on the lawn and the ornamental trees. It was late spring and a breeze was sending spirals of white blossom twisting across the grass. The sky was a sharper, paler blue and the blossom looked whiter than he had seen before. 'Ah, the whitest, frothiest, blossomest blossom', he murmured, aware that his heightened perception was due to the momentous and life-changing nature of his decision.

It was the day after the abortive meeting and his momentous decision to kill Pelham. He was standing at his window and might have been thinking of murder, pubic hair or missing diaries, but instead he was reflecting on the superficiality of university life where one can become known as a 'character' simply by wearing a Stetson hat and burning incense sticks. Apart from some painful memories the hat was the only reminder he had of his brief Texan adventure. He burned incense because he liked the smell and it reminded him of something he couldn't quite recollect. He was waiting for a student to arrive for what he knew was going to be a difficult interview.

On the other side of the lawn, outside Burbanks Hall, Sludge could see his intended victim in animated conversation with two Spanish students (women, of course). 'I wonder if University staff have killed colleagues before.' he thought, 'I know we get away with murder all the time but not your actual killing people. All we tend to destroy is ambition and creativity, but that is through clumsiness and inefficiency rather than intent. Actually that isn't true,' he corrected himself, 'Pelham poisons the minds of his students, and he enjoys it.' He watched with growing fascination as across the campus the students moved nervously, a step here, two steps there, away from Pelham as he moved closer to them, invading their space and forcing a grotesque dance as all three adjusted their positions. 'Are they his next victims?' he wondered, 'It mustn't be. He has to die.'

'Hey, Professor! Who has to die?' Unaware that he had spoken out loud Sludge was startled by a heavily accented voice coming from directly behind him.

'Ah, Fabio,' Sludge had turned to see a tall and slim, dark eyed young man, 'thank you for knocking.' Although his recent attempt to explain the English penchant for irony had been received with utter incomprehension by his non-UK students he still found it impossible to resist. Using the age-old tactic of confidently offering nonsense to detract from his confusion on being overheard he continued, 'No, not die, I said I have fish to fry, Fabio, and you are that fish. Sit down.'

Fabio Brindisi was twenty-two years old and from Naples. His father, Paolo Brindisi, was a lover of all things English with (as Sludge was to discover) the notable exception of the Royal Family who he hated with an unrelenting intensity. Brindisi senior had unspecified international business interests; he also owned two bottling plants and had an interest in several vineyards that his son would inherit in due course. Fabio was in England for a year, ostensibly to get a 'top-up' degree and to improve his English, but he considered it to be a long holiday that was interrupted only by the occasional call into the University. Billy Sludge bothered him. Fabio knew that his family expected him to get his degree, and until he came across Billy Sludge, he had no doubts that he would do just that.

Fabio's degree course was unusual. Designed specifically to attract high fee payers from across Europe it offered a choice of any of the modules offered by the University; choose any ten from two hundred and seventy units and collect a BA Combined Studies degree. This 'pick and mix' approach proved very popular, particularly with less able or lazy students who became adept at choosing the less demanding subjects. As a concession to criticism from the external examiners the University had stopped averaging marks to arrive at a final mark on which to award a degree and had simplified matters by ruling that a pass mark must be obtained in every subject - one failure was enough to fail the entire year.

Fabio had chosen Contemporary African Literature as one of his subjects because he reasoned that few books had been written in Africa and that he could handle Billy Sludge. He was wrong on both counts and suspected that this meeting was to discuss his lack of progress. He recognised his most recent essay, which was on the desk in front of Sludge who had moved from the window and was now sitting facing him.

'Fish? I no fish!' Fabio protested, 'I Italian, from Napoli. You insult me Professor.'

'Thank you for the promotion Fabio but I am not a professor, as you well know. And I was not insulting you; I was using an idiomatic expression. You do know what an idiom is I suppose?' A hostile stare and silence greeted his enquiring look. 'Well, perhaps not.' he shrugged. 'However, that is of no consequence, I called you here to discuss your paper on Alienation in the Post Colonial Literature of Central Southern Africa.'

These were the words that Fabio did not want to hear. Outwardly, his demeanour was relaxed and attentive, but he was very worried. He had read nothing on the subject and his essay was a motley collection of quotes taken randomly from a half-hour exploring the Internet and some material he had stolen from his flatmate's lecture notes. He decided to bluff it out.

'OK, Professor. What you want to know?' he grinned at his interrogator with a cheerfulness he certainly did not feel.

Wearily Sludge looked at the young Italian slumped opposite him. 'Tell me,' he said, passing his hand over his eyes in what he knew was a theatrical gesture of resignation, 'you have written,' he tapped the paper in front of him and read aloud, 'When Marechera commented "I have been an outsider in my own biography" he was acknowledging his hegemonic conditioning, and, in spite of his caustic protestation, "If you are a writer for a specific race or a specific nation, then fuck you", he was ineluctably a Zimbabwean writer.' Sludge paused, inhaled the scent of the sandalwood incense that was burning behind him. 'Tell me,' he continued, ' exactly what do you mean?'

'I mean what I write.' Fabio responded, his sulkiness deepening the natural hoarseness of his voice. 'I mean what I write.' he repeated doing his best to flash his eyes in anger, as he knew Italians were supposed to be able to do. 'What is your problem,' he demanded, 'you no like fuck?'

'On the contrary,' Sludge responded, 'when the opportunity presents itself I very much like fuck. My problem is I don't think you wrote this essay. Now prove me wrong, explain this beautifully written passage. What does it mean?' he repeated.

'What you say?' Fabio widened his eyes in astonishment. 'I no wrote this? How you know I no wrote this?'

Sludge sighed and shook his head. 'I believe that this work is plagiarised.' he said. 'Plagiarism is the passing off of someone else's work as your own.' he responded to Fabio's look of incomprehension. 'The problem is, if that is the case, then you will be awarded zero marks with no opportunity to resit, and you will fail this unit, which means that you will not get a degree. In short you will be off this course and on the next plane back to Italy. Now', he repeated, pushing the papers across the desk, 'take your time and tell me what you mean. If you don't fancy that passage, choose any of the others I have marked. You have a great many to pick from, almost the entire essay in fact. Elaborate on the ideas you have expressed there. In your own words.'

Unhappily Fabio looked down at his essay. Turning the pages slowly he saw that several passages on each page had been highlighted. At first glance it seemed to him that the only parts left unmarked were the few sentences he had actually written himself to link the material he had obtained elsewhere. He had, he realised with regret, badly underestimated his lecturer. Billy Sludge was not the harmless eccentric that was at first indicated by his cowboy hat, his incense sticks and his habit of playing a mouth organ to liven up his lectures. Fabio was a lazy man but not a fool, he knew that Billy Sludge was a hard man; not hard in the way that his father and his father's associates were hard, not hard in a physical way. It was a hardness he hadn't encountered before, more an intellectual toughness, which showed itself as a refusal to accept anything but the best that he thought could be produced. To his horror and shame Fabio began to weep. Hastily wiping a fallen tear from the paper he looked up to see that Sludge had returned to stand at the window.

Moving to the window so that his student could have a private moment to collect himself and appreciate the seriousness of his situation, Sludge saw that Pelham had left the Spanish girls and was now standing in the porch doorway of Burbanks Hall gazing intently across at Carter Hall. Briefly he stepped out of the shadowed doorway and looked left and right before moving quickly back into the shadows from where he pointed directly at Sludge's window. Fascinated, Sludge watched as Pelham moved his other hand over his groin. Waving his pointing hand, and at the same time moving his hips backward and forwards, he jerked his lower hand up and down, simulating a hugely exaggerated masturbation. Then with a final cheery wave and an orgasmic snorting laugh Pelham turned and entered the hall behind him where he knew one of the Spanish girls was waiting for private tuition.

Pelham's laughter came in a series of asthmatic barks as he leaned his back against the door, enjoying his joke. After the meeting yesterday he considered that his problems with Sludge and 'that unfortunate business' were now officially dead and buried. He was aware that Sludge's credibility had taken a beating and suspected that the other man, although more popular, had lost the confidence of some of his supporters. Pelham grinned as he walked down the corridor to his room, thinking that when he was appointed Department Head his first action would be to take over Sludge's room. 'Hello my dear,' he greeted the Spanish girl standing by his door, 'I hope you've prepared for this.' he went on, with the faintest trace of a leer accompanying a series of staccato chortles. The student attempted a polite smile, bit her lip and nodded.

On the other side of the campus Sludge was still standing at his window, he was seeing nothing. The image of the cavorting masturbating monkey Pelham had portrayed had stunned him, had driven everything else out of his mind. Closing his eyes he breathed deeply and held the breath for a count of twenty before releasing it with a low sibilant hiss. Opening his eyes he noticed that the blossom actually had a tinge of grey about it. 'The poisonous bastard', he muttered, 'he's even turned the blossom.'

Suddenly, overwhelmingly, a powerful anger surged through his system and his whole being quivered with a frantic rage brought on by the outrageous behaviour of his colleague. Forgetting everything except his blind passion and sense of impending and inevitable violence, he shook his clenched fist at the building opposite. 'You're going to die.' he screamed, 'You're going to die.'

'Oh, no! Professor!' an anguished Fabio burst out, 'I not die. I admit! I cheat! I cheat. I fucking cheat!' he cried, emphasising his plea by flinging himself forward to crash his head down onto his folded arms. Aghast Sludge looked over his shoulder at the sobbing figure slumped across his desk. Slowly he turned to see a small group of colleagues and students gathering in the open doorway to his room.

'OK,' he said, addressing them with an air of self-possession that was undermined by the fact that his fist was still clenched and above his head, 'nothing to worry about. I can handle this.' With a reassuring smile he closed the door and returned to sit at his desk. He allowed the young Italian several minutes to recover his composure, not only out of compassion but also because he didn't know what to do next. He decided to do nothing until Fabio spoke, he would then react and trust to fortune. 'In the absence of a dice and six options that's all I can do,' he reasoned to himself while regarding the top of Fabio's head. 'I wonder if my hair was ever that thick,' he thought, absently rubbing his hand over his closely cropped hair, an action resulting in a pleasant rasping noise that he found strangely soothing.

THREE

The Albert Bleaney Society - a secret

'It's agreed then, we say nothing about this?' Sludge indicated the small envelope on the centre of the table. 'Nothing at all.'

'I am sure that none of us have a problem with that, Billy.' said Pamela looking across at Joan and Beryl, who both nodded vigorously. 'But what about Scoop? I wonder why he didn't come tonight. Did you tell him about the change of venue?'

'Of course, well at least I left a message on his answer phone.' said Sludge shifting uncomfortably in his chair. The truth is that Sludge had changed the venue from the usual room above the Brickmakers Arms to a small room at the back of the University library without telling Ronan Coyne, whose nickname of Scoop, unbeknown to him because of his justified reputation for throwing quite spectacular tantrums, was due to his technique of wringing every inch of press coverage out of any incident even remotely connected to Albert Bleaney. Not that the Society had suffered from that, but Sludge, who was the one who first referred to him as Scoop, noticed that Ronan always got as much publicity as the late poet. Ronan had also published a book and several articles about the poet and his works. Again, no bad thing thought Sludge, but he suspected that Ronan was driven by self-aggrandisement and the desire to have his efforts recognised, perhaps by a Professorship at his redbrick university.

Inspired by his friendship with the poet Sludge had written some poems but had not tried to have them published. He had a vague intention to write about Albert Bleaney at some time. He was also thinking about a novel, but was having problems getting past that certain knowing approach that declares, 'I know everyone thinks they can write a novel - here is mine, I really can'. When a young man Sludge had read that every young person secretly knows that they are going to be famous. The article had depressed him greatly as he did secretly know just that. He did not want to produce a work making capital out of exposing the futile dreams of the many, at least that is what he told himself. His real fear was that he didn't have anything to say that was worth the effort.

Alarmed by the possibilities open to Ronan if he learned of the salacious titbit found in the house, Sludge had manipulated his absence from the meeting and secured the promise of secrecy from the others. Joan and Beryl, who each knew that her own pubic hair was intact but now wondered about the other, had been horrified and, concerned for their 'good name', were only too happy to agree to a pact of silence.

'The fewer people that know the better it is.' Sludge said, ' We should keep the information between the four of us. There is no reason to tell Scoop anything at all about our discovery. I will take possession of it, and dispose of it. We should then forget it ever existed. Agreed?'

'Yes.' said Pamela.

'Yes.' said Beryl.

Joan was gazing intently at the envelope. She looked up at the others, 'Yes, yes, I agree. Say nothing and get rid of it is the best way. But,' she paused, 'I don't think that Albert wrote these numbers, he never crossed his sevens in that fashion.' She tapped the envelope with a forefinger 'And I remember the date, seventeenth July 1985.' The room was suddenly very quiet as the elderly woman looked pensively at the centre of the table. 'He asked me to go with him. At first I agreed, but I changed my mind because of some silly argument. Anyway I stayed at home and he went alone. The seventeenth of July 1985, that was the day he went to Buckingham Palace to receive his OBE.'

A visit to the coast

Driving out to the coast that evening after the Albert Bleaney Society committee meeting, Sludge reflected on Fabio's eventual response. The young Italian had remained silent for several minutes before he had surprised and impressed Sludge by presenting a calm and accurate summary of his predicament. He asked for time to discuss his problems with his father and promised to return within forty-eight hours to discuss his options. 'Options? What options?' Sludge mused as his car crested a rise giving the driver a view of the small coastal town of Shrivellsea, a place he had disliked at first sight. It was, he had decided after that first desultory visit, borrowing a phrase from his father, 'a place of piss-ups and paper-hats.' When Peter Pelham bought his 'luxury flat' there a couple of years ago Sludge had concluded that the tasteless two, the town and the man, just about deserved each other. Pelham was the reason for his current excursion.

Sitting in his car with the engine idling, Sludge watched the rain drift through the streetlights. It was at times like this that he regretted that he did not smoke cigarettes. He mimed the act of a smoker, sucked pensively on a non-existent Marlboro (probably Marlboro although, 'Can you buy them here?' he puzzled) before winding down the window to flick the butt arching through the drizzle to land with a defiant sizzle in the red and blue reflections of neon on the wet road. He loved this weather. As a boy he had roamed the streets of his hometown with his coat collar turned up against the weather, poetry in his head and a romantic notion of destiny in his heart. 'On the other side of a gulf well-nigh incredible,' he pronounced gravely, his voice booming inside the car, 'He watched a uniformed and bearded king place with a kid-gloved hand a wreath of flowers at the foot of a cenotaph gleaming whitely under the pale blue of a London winter sky.'

He cupped the glowing end of another Marlboro in his curled fist, and blew a long stream of blue smoke against the windscreen, making it mist over. Watching it become clear he announced slowly and precisely, enunciating each word carefully, 'I was as a child but when I became a man I put away childish things.' Slumping in his seat he lisped a North American drawl, 'I coulda been a contender Charlie, I coulda been a contender.' Sludge sat up quickly as he noticed that someone had just left the Magpie and Stump public house - his breathing sharpened as he recognised Poisonous Pete. 'Welcome to my nightmare, O poisonous one.' Sludge muttered as he eased the car into gear.

The engine threatened to cut out as he played the clutch up and down trying to keep the speed below walking pace. 'A ten year old rust-bucket Escort with 95,000 miles on the clock is not really up to this job.' he thought gloomily. His original intention had been to obtain, somehow, an old Citroen with a running board or, failing that, a large black Mercedes with a gun- sight badge on the bonnet. Silently the large black car slid in and out of the shadows, slipped around corners, moved effortlessly under the hand of the cold eyed driver who was wearing a long black leather coat, rumoured to be the very same coat worn by James Mason as Field Marshal Rommel in *The Desert Fox*. He had travelled this route many times and, pulling ahead of the tall striding figure he was following, he accelerated. His quarry was a man of habit. He visited the same places, walked the same streets, and returned home to his third floor flat, where every night he stood in the window looking out at the North Sea. The cold-eyed driver left the Mercedes a hundred yards or so from the mansion flats. He was now standing on the beach in the shadow of the sea wall. Looking up at the flats, he screwed the silencer onto the extended barrel of his Buntline Special, a unique firearm made to his exact specifications and a faithful copy of the Buntline used by Sheriff Pat Garrett, with 21st century modifications of course. His quarry was home; standing in the window offering a target the cold-eyed gunman couldn't miss. Resting his arm on the sea wall he took careful aim at the silhouetted figure. Gently he exhaled as he slowly squeezed…

'Shit! Shit! Shit!' Sludge exploded. 'Shit and fucking shit!' In attempting to keep up with Pelham, but not be seen, Sludge's car had mounted the pavement and the Escort was now nestling snugly between a lamppost and a garden wall. Unable to open either door Sludge peered about him. He couldn't see Pelham anywhere, however he did notice several people appeared to have left the house immediately on his left and were staring at him through the windscreen. One of them, a woman of indeterminate age, but an obviously violent disposition, was shouting and gesticulating. As far as Sludge could make out she was repeating the word 'pervert' over and over again with an increasing ferocity.

FOUR

'Dr Ludgeworth I presume?'

The Brickmakers Arms was an old fashioned public house before it was acquired by a multi national conglomerate with an interest in buying such places and converting them to 'olde worlde eateries'. The wooden floor had been replaced with laminate strips, and the open fire replaced with a living-flame gas fire so real that only someone paying attention would notice the difference. Renaming was part of the authentication policy and The Brickmakers was now, rather strangely, but no doubt authentically, The Fox and Goose, a name everyone ignored. Standing directly opposite the university, 'Brickies', as it was still known, was a regular meeting place for the academic staff. By tacit agreement students kept out of Brickies and patronised either the student bar on campus, a black hell hole serving watery beer in plastic tumblers, or went into the town to one of the few student-friendly establishments to be served watery beer in made-in-Taiwan tankards.

Brickies had some claim as Albert Bleaney's local and for that reason the Society held their monthly meetings there in an upstairs room. Nostalgia wasn't the only reason; Harry Cooper the landlord had fond memories of the poet and made no charge for the room. For a number of years Sludge and Albert had met in the bar every Saturday lunchtime and Harry, who was a crossword devotee, often asked for their advice on the more tricky clues as he attempted the prize crossword in *The Independent*. He also had a framed photograph behind the bar showing himself and the poet inspecting a copy of *Newts*, the controversial poem linking the life of the small amphibian with the drinking habits of literary critics. The

Society had a notice board in the entrance foyer and on his way in Sludge saw that a tall young man wearing a green Barbour jacket was studying the notices very closely and appeared to be making a note of the details of the Ottingham walk. Only someone much more observant than Sludge would have also seen that the tall young man was taking a keen interest in Sludge himself.

It was five days after the disastrous excursion to Shrivellsea and Sludge was sitting at a table in the window recess of the Hunters Bar overlooking the rear garden. He turned away from watching a song thrush feeding two of its young and glanced across at the bar where Desiree Croucher was ordering their drinks. Standing next to the Dean a tall thin man with sunken cheeks and a thick drooping moustache leaned back, looking around the room. Wearing a long black coat that was hanging open, the man supported himself on the bar with his elbows behind him, his hands dangling by his sides. Sludge met his eyes briefly and was momentarily disconcerted by the blank stare. Shifting his gaze, Sludge looked at Croucher's back, the number of shoulder straps quite clearly visible under her bright white nylon blouse puzzled him. He could count four, all different colours, on each shoulder. 'Why so many? What do they all do? Are they part of an elaborate support system designed to keep all that flesh in order?' he pondered. Suddenly visions of concealed guns or recording devices alarmed him. 'I wonder if she is armed or wired for sound?' he asked himself. He did not know why Desiree had asked him for a 'bit of a chat'; perhaps she intended to quiz him and get his responses on tape. He considered the bulky figure at the bar, 'Never mind a microphone, you could conceal a complete audio system in those pink acres.' he mused. His cold eyes narrowed to little more than slits as his gaze flicked around the saloon, he could sense danger in the air. Tilting his Stetson hat forward he leaned back in his chair and crossed his black booted feet over his outstretched ankles. He must be vigilant but they must not know. His right hand on the butt of his revolver, his senses taut, his body coiled and ready to spring into action, he feigned sleep.

Holding his pint of Guinness an inch or two from his mouth Sludge looked around the room, 'I don't really like this place,' he said gloomily 'I never did.' he added before his companion could blame the conversion. Actually Desiree Croucher had no intention of being drawn into discussing the merits or otherwise of old-pub conversions. She had asked Sludge for this informal drink so that she could be prepared for the formal disciplinary meeting that the Vice - Chancellor had called, and in which Sludge, although he didn't yet know it, was to be the star turn. Desiree was anxious to help Sludge, but had become increasingly concerned at his behaviour in recent months; the business with Pelham had dragged on too long and had obviously unsettled him and now there was this other business. She had prepared for this meeting by deciding to take a direct approach.

Desiree Croucher, Dean of the Faculty, was very concerned. Sludge was a respected, if, according to some, a somewhat eccentric and sometimes misguided, member of the University. But the gradual personality change she thought she had noticed take effect following the death of his brother, and then his parents, seemed to be escalating as he became increasingly preoccupied and, in her words, 'distant and semi-detached'.

Some days ago, the police and the fire brigade had been called out to rescue him from an angry mob besieging him in his car that had somehow become trapped on the pavement, wedged between a lamppost and a garden wall. A section of the wall had had to be demolished to release the car and driver. Unfortunately the area where the incident had taken place had become notorious in recent months due to an influx of 'ladies of the night' (and all other hours it should be said). Even more unfortunately the garden wall belonged to the local leader of a movement whose aim was to discourage cruising motorists who were keen to support this new (to the area) and enterprising economic initiative. Sludge stood accused by the local people of being a 'kerb-crawler', and, it was possible, by the police of driving without due care and attention, and conduct likely to lead to a breach of the peace.

The Vice Chancellor, Professor Max Badowski, was a kindly man of Polish extraction with thick black hair hanging in an untidy fringe, almost meeting the large and bushy beard which crept up his face to the bags under his eyes, giving the impression that he was for ever peeping out of a particularly dense undergrowth. Professor Badowski, who, although somewhat unworldly and a sociologist, was nevertheless a clear thinker and decisive, had told Dean Croucher to, 'Find out what is wrong with Ludgeworth. He hasn't been the same since that dreadful incident with the Japanese girl. He is a good man and too valuable to lose. We want to help him if we can.' He had advised her that the disciplinary meeting was a necessary formality and although he was far from certain that it was possible, he wanted a rescue operation. He explained that he was not prepared to abandon Sludge, but conceded that he may have placed himself 'beyond help'. Privately Dean Croucher was not convinced that the Vice Chancellor knew what he was talking about; if Sludge was out of the way then life, although probably less interesting would certainly be quieter. Her own agenda featuring the drive to increase recruitment by imposing less exacting standards would benefit from the removal of its most vociferous opponent, and, of course, the promotion of Pelham would be so much smoother. She had a difficult path to tread; above all she mustn't do anything that could endanger her own standing with the Vice Chancellor.

'William,' she smiled across at Sludge, 'we have been friends for a long time. I'm very worried about you. You are in some trouble with the university and, quite possibly, with the police.' Leaning forward, and with admirable dexterity, she pursed her lips, pushed her tongue into her cheek, half closed one eye, and nodded briskly several times in conspiratorial fashion. 'Please,' she composed her face and smiled again, 'you can tell me. Why were you in that part of Shrivellsea? What were you doing to get the car in that position?' She sat back, smiled encouragingly for a third time, and waited for Sludge to respond. It was with some relief that Sludge realised the reason for the meeting, her questions confirmed to him that he was under surveillance, but he had been half-afraid that Desiree fancied him and was going to make him an offer he wouldn't accept.

'Because. Because. Because.' Sludge said. He sighed and looked across at the bar where his attention was again caught by the long, lean man in black who was still staring at him. Somewhat distracted, he turned to the window where he observed that a large black and white cat had concealed itself in the bushes at the edge of the now, thankfully, bird-free lawn. Anxiously he looked around, but could see no sign of the thrush family. He didn't want to talk about his motoring misadventure; he had only accepted Desiree's invitation because it was the first time for weeks that anyone had behaved in a friendly fashion toward him. Drawing deeply on an imaginary Marlboro he regarded the woman coldly as she waited eagerly for his reply, he knew she was going to be disappointed, but, 'Hell! Join the club.' he muttered under his breath.

The silence hung between the pair like a cloud that also muffled all other sounds from the room. Sludge could hear, as from a distance, but really from the speaker over his head, a country voice singing. He caught the words, 'I was all right for a while. I could smile for a while.' and grinned. He loved those somebody-done-me-wrong songs. Movement in the garden caught his attention and he turned to see that that thrush had returned and was once more feeding her young. There was no sign of the cat. On turning back to the table he was shocked to find Desiree's face was now no more than six inches from his.

'William,' Desiree began, with all the authority a university Dean could muster, 'Let me explain this to you very simply.' She had pulled her chair as close as possible and heaved her breasts on to the table so that she could lean further across. Ignoring the look of alarm on Sludge's face she went on, 'You are in deep shit. You are to attend a formal disciplinary meeting. Your livelihood is at stake. I'm here to help you, but you must help me to do that. Now,' she continued emphatically, 'tell me, what is going on? I know Pelham lives in Shrivellsea - was this ridiculous caper somehow connected with your vendetta against him? Tell me,' she demanded, 'I want to help you, for God's sake.' Reaching across to grasp his arm she pursed her lips several times in quick succession then rolled her tongue around her cheek, nodding vigorously at the same time, 'Tell me.' she insisted. Withdrawing slightly Desiree released her grip on Sludge's arm and looked into his eyes while she began again the lip pursing and tongue rolling routine that she imagined indicated her sincerity and confidentiality. Why she thought that is unclear, but it is true to state that those facial actions never failed to have an impact. In this instance the impact, and the repercussions of that, were quite spectacular.

Spellbound by Desiree's facial gymnastics, Sludge was also very puzzled. What was she doing with her face? So far he had been spared the breast heaving and sniffing - although why she had tossed her frighteningly large breasts onto the table where there lay quivering at him, he did not know - but what was this business with the face? Why was she gurning at him? Surely she wasn't trying to flirt with him in some strange ritual known only to senior female academics. Discreetly he tried to imitate his companion's facial contortions, but succeeded only in biting on the very tip of his tongue. Quickly disguising his involuntary yelp of pain into a coughing spasm he patted his chest while trying a reassuring smile. An attempt rather undermined by the streaks of blood rapidly appearing on his teeth, and the thin trickle of blood and saliva beginning to run from the side of his mouth. Turning his head to wipe his mouth, Sludge was horrified to see that the cat was concealed in the bushes from where it was staring, with an obviously malicious intent, at the thrush family. Quickly he took a mouthful of Guinness to clear the inside of his mouth only to find that his throat had gone into spasm and he couldn't swallow. At that moment the cat ran across the lawn and pounced on one of the young thrushes. Aghast Sludge leaped from his seat shouting as he did so and thereby projecting a gory mixture of Guinness and blood against the window from where it rebounded to splatter the face and bright white nylon blouse of Desiree Croucher.

Out on the lawn Sludge looked around him, there was no trace of the cat or the thrushes. He could see Desiree's horrified and bloody face staring at him through the window. The cold-eyed man allowed the thin line of blood to run down his chin unchecked. He concentrated on the pain from his wound to keep his mind clear. He could see that his companion was unsettled and that was good.

The cadaverous man in black had followed Sludge outside and now walked towards him, one hand outstretched the other carrying a large black hat with a silver band, 'Dr Ludgeworth, I presume? I've always wanted to say that.' His mouth smiled, but his eyes didn't. 'Unfortunately my name isn't Stanley, but as yours isn't Livingstone, nothing lost there.' Bewildered, Sludge's attempts to question this odd introduction were severely hampered by his inability to control his tongue.

'Ah,' continued the man in black, 'I did want a talk but I see that it would be advisable to delay that for a little while. If I may suggest,' he adopted a solicitous air and briefly touched his own tongue, 'some ice would do the trick in no time. Here is my card, I'm staying locally.' Sludge glanced at the card; there was a name, John Henry Holliday MD, and an address, which read c/o The Boulderado Hotel, Boulder, Colorado. There was nothing else.

Grasping Sludge's arm with a surprisingly strong grip the stranger smiled, 'I represent the interests of Paulo Brindisi here in England,' with his forefinger he drew a circle above his head, before adding enigmatically, 'and elsewhere. You know his son, Fabio.' He inclined his head, accepting Sludge's nodded agreement. 'Signor Brindisi is most anxious to assist you in resolving the difficulties you are experiencing with his only, and dearly loved son. We need to talk soon, very soon. I'll be in touch. We must meet. By the way,' he went on, 'do you know you are being watched?'

Releasing his grip he stared at Sludge for several seconds as he carefully replaced his hat, the large brim shadowing his eyes, before turning slowly and walking away. Heading back through the bar he nodded and touched his hat in mock salute to a tall athletic looking young man wearing a green Barbour jacket and grinned as the other immediately turned his back.

Approaching Dean Croucher Dr Holliday removed his hat and placed it carefully on the table, 'A most unfortunate and regrettable incident.' he said. 'Dr Ludgeworth is, of course, quite ill. Problems with perspective,' he said enigmatically as he gazed steadily at the bewildered, blood and Guinness spattered Dean, 'I am going to help him.' he said. 'I am aware that he is in difficulties already and it would be best if this incident did not complicate matters. It will be best for him, best for the University, and,' he reached for her hand which he held a shade too firmly, 'best for you, if this,' sweeping his arm he somehow encompassed both her discomfort and the past ten minutes, 'is allowed to pass without comment. '

Releasing her hand he retrieved his hat, inspected it for traces of blood and Guinness and finding none, placed it on his head. Adjusting the brim so that it shadowed his eyes, he held his unsmiling gaze on the speechless Dean.

'Best for everyone.' he said placing a finger to his lips before turning and walking quickly from the room.

FIVE

A question of discipline

As Director of Personnel at the University Leo McFee was concerned only with staffing matters and was secretly relieved that he had no official contact with the student body. A large fat Scotsman with small dark eyes set in a spotty, pasty face topped by a very neat 1960s Beatle fringe, McFee, although recognised as part of 'management', was known only to the students as a figure of fun. His rare appearances as he pigeon-toed speedily about the campus, head thrust forward to balance his huge backside were always greeted with quacking noises, which he didn't understand, but suspected were insulting. The students, if they referred to him at all, called him 'that fat bloke' or 'Spotted Dick', following an incident in the refectory when a student had looked at his raisin spattered pudding and shouted, 'Christ, I'm eating that fat bloke's face'.

McFee disliked the title Director of Personnel; it was he thought, too suggestive of staff welfare and people concerns. He had argued for 'Personnel' to be replaced with 'Human Resource Management'. With its emphasis on strategic planning, a matter of getting the right person in the right place at the right time, it was, he considered, more suited to his personality. He was well aware that he was a numbers person rather than a people person. McFee had entered his chosen profession because he reasoned that the Thatcher years, followed by the Major years and the Blair years, by under funding the universities, and rewarding a macho management style, had produced an environment in which the ruthless could prosper. In this he had badly underestimated the style of the academic leader, a style that was long on discussion and short on any sort of action. A frustrated man who felt, quite rightly, that he had achieved little in his four years at the University, McFee viewed the forthcoming disciplinary interview with Dr William Ludgeworth as an opportunity for him to make a mark. He knew he had the support of Dean Croucher and had been pleased when Dr Peter Pelham had purposely sought him out to offer his unequivocal support.

The Vice Chancellor had a large room in the oldest part of the University; with its stone fireplace, book-lined walls, rosewood desk at one end and a small matching table and four leather armchairs at the other, it was, according to McFee, too 'cosy' to be conducive to business decision making. McFee looked across the table. 'We have a chance,' he pointed out to Vice Chancellor Badowski and Desiree Croucher as they waited for the unfortunate Sludge, ' to be seen to be taking decisive and punitive action that will serve *pour encourager les autres*.'

The Vice Chancellor had a sociologist's disdain for pretension and winced at both McFee's pronunciation and the sentiment behind his portentous pronouncement. Unhappily he peered through his tangled mass of hair and beard as McFee continued. 'You know that our staffing costs are too high. This is an opportunity too good to miss. However you look at it, Ludgeworth is guilty of gross misconduct, you must sack him'. In the uncomfortable silence that followed he sensed that Badowski was not convinced. 'I don't see what the problem is', he persisted, 'we have a campus staffed by free loaders and the walking wounded. Here is a gilt edged opportunity to move one out. We must do that. It is important that we send out the right signals.'

'You haven't said much Desiree,' the Vice Chancellor said, 'what is your view? Are we peopled by free loaders and the walking wounded?'

It was the day after her calamitous meeting with Sludge and Dean Croucher was still shaken. Apart from being covered in blood and Guinness, the tall man with the hat and faint American accent had also unsettled her. Exactly what did he know about Sludge and why, she wondered, would it be best for her to keep quiet about his extraordinary behaviour? And yet she had no doubt that she would keep quiet. There was something about the man, in his eyes or the way he had gripped her hand, that convinced her that it would be against her interests to reveal any details whatsoever. Dean Croucher had experience only of dealing with academics and to come face to face with such unambiguous intent and surety of purpose was new to her, and very unsettling. Though she did not know the man, neither his intentions nor his purpose, she had decided not only to keep quiet, but also to soft pedal during the imminent interview.

Dean Croucher took a deep breath before replying, 'We have some people who may need some encouragement, but reference to our staff as free loaders and the walking wounded is going too far.' she said to the utter astonishment of McFee who had expected her to favour his approach. A not unreasonable expectation following their earlier conversations in which she had appeared to share his philosophy of the need for 'a flexible workforce' in which a quantifiable 'bottom line' is the critical factor, not the uncountable and unaccountable 'quality of the university experience' some appeared to support. Ignoring the (she thought) theatrical gasp from McFee she addressed herself to the Vice Chancellor, 'William Ludgeworth is a valued member of staff, a little misguided at times, and no doubt eccentric at others, but he has done valuable work in the past and, with suitable encouragement, will do so again.'

'Quite. Quite.' murmured Vice Chancellor Badowski, pleased to have the support he had asked for, but puzzled by its fulsomeness. 'However the decision may be taken out of our hands if the police decide to prosecute, as I understand they might. The Board of Governors have told me that a successful prosecution would make Ludgeworth's position here untenable. I had of course given them the brief facts, as I must, but it appears that they have since received a great deal more detailed information about Ludgeworth and his activities. From you I understand Leo. Can you confirm that?' He did not bother to hide the distaste he felt for the political manoeuvrings of his Director of Personnel. Distaste he felt acquiring a personal edge as he watched the man's bloated features blotch red with embarrassment. 'In the circumstances,' he continued as McFee failed to respond, 'I consider that we have no alternative other then to suspend Ludgeworth until the police have settled on a course of action. What happens as a result of that action will determine Ludgeworth's future here.'

At that moment a small dark woman entered the room after a brief rap on the door. 'Excuse me, Vice Chancellor,' she said, 'Dr Ludgeworth is here.'

'Ask him to wait please, Veronica,' he replied, still looking at McFee, 'just for a couple of minutes.'

Veronica nodded and left the room. After closing the door behind her she looked across at Sludge. 'They'll be just a couple of minutes. Please take a seat. I hope you don't mind, but I've got to get on with this.' She pointed to a large pile of papers on her desk.

Sludge smiled and lifted his hand, 'That's OK' he said, lisping slightly due to the injury to his tongue, as he took a chair near the window. Once more the cold-eyed man concentrated on his pain. He liked the way it sharpened his mind. They were waiting for him, but he was ready. He looked across the campus and liked what he saw. He'd been happy here, but, he drew heavily on his Marlboro cigarette, maybe it was time to move on, settle the unfinished business, and move on.

McFee moved uneasily on the low armchair, his bulk squeaking against the leather with short sharp farting noises. 'I had no choice;' he said, 'the Chairman of the Board asked me questions and I answered them.'

'In full and glorious detail, no doubt.' said the Vice Chancellor who broke the ensuing short silence by continuing, 'Well, it is done now. But not forgotten. I will talk to you further following the meeting. Do you have anything to add Desiree?' Stunned by the sudden speed with which events had moved, Dean Croucher shook her head.

'In that case ask Billy to come in McFee'. The familiar use of Ludgeworth's first name contrasting with the harsh formality of his own surname made a point not lost on McFee, who, he comforted himself, was prepared to concede some rather meaningless ground, sensing that he was on the way to winning a battle.

McFee, who found the low armchairs most awkward and uncomfortable, had sat back further than he intended and found it rather difficult to lever himself into an upright position. Leaning forward, he placed his hands on the small table. However, as soon as he transferred his weight the table tipped towards him causing the Vice Chancellor's coffee cup to slide off the table and crash to the floor. In his attempt to catch the cup, McFee lurched further forward and slipped off the chair onto his knees. From this position he was able to consider his options. For a man of his size springing lightly to his feet was not one of them; neither was another attempt at leaning on the table. Turning to face the chair he gripped the arms and began to heave himself erect. To his great discomfort, the chair began to roll away from him, slowly at first, but with increasing speed as his weight became a propelling force acting on the motion of the chair. With a spryness that surprised everyone in the room, not least of all himself, he got off his knees. Unfortunately, the chair was now too far away from him for the angle between his feet and outstretched arms to be sustained. The speeding chair hit the bookcase with a thump but not before McFee had been forced to release his grip. He now lay face down on the carpet.

'Stop horsing around McFee.' came the strangely strangled tones of the Vice Chancellor as Dean Croucher struggled with a sudden spasm of coughing, 'Go and get Billy.'

The cold-eyed man looked up sharply as the office door opened. It was the fat bloke. He hadn't expected him. 'Come in Ludgeworth.' McFee grunted, his crimson face streaked with perspiration, 'Come in.'

Slowly and deliberately the cold-eyed man extinguished his cigarette between forefinger and thumb and dropped the butt into a plant pot on the window sill, then, his right hand on the butt of his revolver, he strolled forward to face the showdown. He was calm, he was cold, and he was ready.

We can handle anything

'I am suspended until the police decide what to do. Apparently, Badowski has been advised that formal charges are almost a certainty due to pressure on the police to be seen to be doing something about problems in that god-forsaken hole. If they prosecute successfully, then I will be dismissed. If the prosecution is unsuccessful it is unlikely that I could stay on, even if I wanted to, which is doubtful.'

Sludge was sitting on a bench looking across the library lawn. He was talking to Dr Holliday who appeared to have been waiting for him when he left the Vice Chancellor's office.

'Tell me,' he went on, 'is your name really Dr Holliday? And are you really from Boulder, Colorado?'

'Call me Doc.' said the man with a grin. 'What my name is and where I am from doesn't really matter. You are a fan of Bob Dylan I understand? You will remember that when asked to explain his sometimes-obscure lyrics he refused and told his questioner that his lyrics meant what you wanted them to mean. With that in mind, I can be anyone you like and from anywhere you choose. All you have to accept is that I am here to help you to help Fabio. All you need to know is that my friends, and me, we can handle anything. When does your suspension start?'

Sludge looked up at the clock above the library entrance. 'In thirty minutes,' he said. 'McFee wanted to escort me from the premises there and then, but Badowski overruled him. I have until 4.00 o'clock to take what I need from my room and to leave the campus. After that I cannot come back onto the campus, or communicate with anyone from the University, colleagues or students, until my suspension is lifted, or...'

He paused as two final year students approached and greeted him with a friendly, 'How're you doing Dr Sludge?'

'I'm doing fine,' Sludge grinned, 'just fine. How are you doing?'

'I guess things could be better.' The taller of the two said, stepping forward to hold his hand out to Sludge, 'Hang on in there Billy. You're one of the good guys. OK?'

Shaking the young man's hand Sludge nodded. 'OK. You're not so bad yourself Danny.' he said. 'Unfortunately, unlike your famous cousin Rocky I can't claim that 'Somebody up there likes me', but I'll get by'.

Danny Graziano smiled at the reference to Rocky Graziano. He wasn't actually related to the former light middle weight boxing world champion, in fact the first time he had heard of the boxer was when Sludge suggested that he bore some resemblance to Rocky Graziano as portrayed in the film starring Paul Newman, and titled *Somebody Up There Likes Me*.

After watching the pair walk away the cold-eyed man turned to the man from Colorado, 'or, as I was saying,' he continued, 'I am forced to ride off into the sunset'.

'Do they know?' Doc Holliday nodded in the direction of the retreating students having observed the obviously affectionate though brief exchange with interest.

'I think everyone knows about the Shrivellsea fiasco, but it will take until tomorrow morning for the suspension to become general knowledge. Sorry Doc,' he said glancing up at the clock, 'I have things to do, I have to go.'

'Before you do,' he said, placing his hand on Sludge's arm, 'please forgive my narrow field of interest, but where exactly does this leave Fabio Brindisi?'

The cold-eyed man smiled a thin smile. Squinting against the smoke curling up from his Marlboro cigarette he coolly regarded the Doc. Fabio Brindisi was a good kid but he was through. He had risked everything on one throw and he had lost. The cold-eyed man knew he could have helped him, but that was before his own troubles rode into town.

'You must understand,' said Sludge, 'Fabio submitted an illegal work that deserves to fail. One failure and he's off the course. Having said that I do know that Fabio is a lazy student rather than a dishonest one.'

Removing the other's hand from his arm, he stood up. 'I would have encouraged him to submit another piece of work, his own this time. He made a mistake, but I don't think he deserves to pay such a heavy price. Unfortunately I am suspended and cannot help him now. He has to live with what he has done.'

'Not if your suspension is cancelled.' Doc Holliday said quietly, looking up at the weathervane on the roof of

Burbanks Hall as it slowly turned in the light breeze that had just appeared.

'That will take weeks.' said Sludge, 'If it is lifted at all.'

'I need twenty-four hours. Today is Thursday - we need to meet on Saturday.'

'Twenty four hours to do what?' Sludge was puzzled.

'To get your suspension lifted. You really don't know who you are dealing with, do you?' The man stood up and grinned as he removed his hat to run his fingers through his hair. 'I told you, my friends and me, we can do anything, anything at all. I'll join you on the Bleaney Walk, we can discuss things then.'

Half turned to walk away, the breeze blowing his long coat open, he added almost as an afterthought, 'Don't worry Billy; this isn't going to be a repeat of the Texas experience. The young man was right, you're one of the good guys, and you've got friends. Friends down here, and in my experience they are a lot more practical than anything you'll get from up there.' he said pointing to the Heavens.

Unable to grasp the implications of this sudden development, and lost in thought, Sludge watched the retreating figure of his enigmatic 'friend' before, with a deep sigh, he set off for his room.

'It's four o'clock Ludgeworth.' McFee was standing in the doorway of Sludge's room, rubbing his hands together. He was very eager to see the man off the premises.

Pelham had accompanied McFee on his mission to see Sludge escorted from the campus and had been standing out of sight, but he now stepped forward into the doorway and looked around the room with deliberate slowness. 'Nice room this,' he murmured, 'good views,' he nodded at the window, 'I'll be very comfortable in here. Anything I can do to help you on your way?'

In the absence of a witty response, Sludge simply said, 'One minute.' as he kicked the door shut in the faces of the gloating Director of Personnel and the egregious Pelham.

The cold-eyed man sat down tilting his chair back so that he could lift his booted feet onto the desk. How come the man from Colorado knew about Texas, he mused. He knew other things too, knew he liked Bob Dylan for instance. How did he know that? What else did he know? Who was this stranger and who are his friends? Could they really help? Blowing a thin stream of blue smoke at the ceiling the cold-eyed man saw the unfinished business with Poisonous Pete swim into view and felt a depression beginning to grip him. 'Fuck off black dog' he muttered.

He picked up his bag and looped it over his shoulder. Pausing for a moment Sludge looked around the room before opening the door. The cold-eyed man saw that McFee was now alone. 'OK, fat boy', he said, 'let's get this over with.' His hand resting lightly on the butt of his revolver, he strolled down the corridor. Irritated by the fat bloke's laboured breathing, Sludge ran down the stairs and out of the building. Crossing the campus at a very fast walk Sludge left the University grounds. He didn't look back.

SIX

Nowhere and nothing

Sludge had been at the University of the East Riding for less than a year when Sheila McKechnie joined him having secured a non-contract post teaching English literature. An ebullient Irishwoman, Sheila's habit of shouting, 'Hello, Billy Sludge!' whenever she spotted him as she cycled about the campus on an ancient sit-up-and-beg bicycle endeared her to the students, but raised critical eyebrows in some sections of the Faculty. Sludge's inevitable reaction to the shouted greeting, which was to doff his hat with a wide sweeping gesture and to bow from the waist, endorsed his growing reputation, both as an eccentric and as an 'all-right-bloke'. It also signalled his general acceptance of the soubriquet, which now had a permanent air as it was passed on by successive generations of students, its origins lost in time.

They had met as postgraduate students, and it was only due to family commitments and her unfinished doctoral thesis that Sheila didn't go to America with Sludge. At first they lived in the Avenues, an area much favoured by University types, but they soon tired of the incestuous nature of life there and moved to a spacious flat at the top of a Victorian house overlooking a park. When Sheila eventually accepted a senior post teaching post-colonial literature at the University of Aarhus in Denmark it was agreed that he would follow 'in due course'. Little more than a year after Sheila's move his mother died, and Sludge found himself an only child and an orphan at the age of thirty-nine. Sheila had been at Aarhus seven years now and her once frequent visits to England were marked by an increasingly lengthy period of time between each one. Sludge still hadn't been to Aarhus and, truth to tell, had accepted that it was unlikely that he would ever go there.

Sludge liked the house, he appreciated the confidence of the Victorians who erected substantial buildings, designed to last. He particularly liked his flat; the deep dormer windows attracted him, so deep that he could stand in the recess looking out over a row of horse chestnut trees that fringed the park opposite. Standing there now with a glass of white wine, which he sipped carefully mindful of the damage to his tongue, he was reviewing the events of that afternoon. Watching the evening sky darken to match his mood, his thoughts turned to Albert Bleaney who had visited this flat many times. Softly, Sludge spoke aloud the final stanza from *Dormer Windows*.

I thought of dormer windows.
Beyond the glass the night,
Beyond the night
Nowhere and nothing.

'Nowhere and nothing,' he repeated as he refilled his glass from the bottle on the small table at his side, 'that just about sums up my situation.' Leaning out of the open window he raised his glass to the trees opposite, 'Begone dull care! I prithee begone from me.' With melodramatic emphasis he drained his glass before throwing it into the garden thirty feet below for it to land in a large shrub.

If Sludge had been looking out of his window a few moments later he would have seen a tall young man wearing a green Barbour jacket emerge from the shelter of the trees and walk cautiously across the road. The man entered the garden and retrieved the undamaged wine glass, which he inspected thoughtfully before looking up at Sludge's window. Carefully he picked his way across the garden, heading towards the door of the house.

Sludge was not looking out of his window. Satisfied with his gesture and crossing his arms in front of his chest he began to bounce on the balls of his feet while sticking out his bottom lip in a crude imitation of the Italian dictator Benito Mussolini, 'April is-a-da cruellest month.' he said attempting a singsong Italian accent. Relaxing his pose, he turned away from the window. 'It looks as though May is going to be a bit of a bastard as well.' he said gloomily.

'Everything seems lovely, when you start to roam', he sang as he suddenly sashayed across the room, 'things won't seem so lovely when you're on your own, here's what you'll be saying when you're far from home.' Dropping down onto one knee he clasped his hands to his chest before throwing his arms wide and singing very loudly, 'Mammy! My little Mammy! The sun shines east, the sun shines west.' Abruptly Sludge stopped singing and sat on the floor.

He remembered his elder brother Eddie singing that song at the party to celebrate his parent's Silver Wedding. Eddie, seven years older than Sludge, was twenty-three at the time and hadn't known all the words; instead he kept singing over and over again, 'This is my mammy I'm talking about nobody else's mammy.' Eddie had died suddenly aged thirty-five the year after Sludge returned from America; both his parents, devastated by the death of their eldest son, had died within five years. At Eddie's funeral his mother, who was an Al Jolson fan insisted on playing a record of Jolson singing *Sonny Boy*. 'Not a dry eye in the house, kiddo.' said Sludge, holding his knees and rocking gently back and forth as he wept.

Sludge had suffered from a depressive illness since childhood, although it hadn't been diagnosed as such until adulthood. As a child his occasional moods of extreme anxiety followed by a numbing depression had been diagnosed either as 'nerves' or 'growing pains', with a consequent lack of any treatment other than being sent to stay for a few days with one of his mum's sisters. When he was eighteen, about to go up to university he graduated from visits to his Aunt to mild medication, and it was only when in his late twenties that a sympathetic GP had resisted the easy route of prescribing pills. Alarmed by Sludge's admitted attraction to 'the appealing comfort of the blanket of oblivion' his doctor, being unsure whether Sludge was seeking the dreamless sanctity offered by suicide, or the deceptive visions inspired by alcohol, took the cautious view and referred him to a psychotherapist. Several sessions of the 'talking cure' had informed Sludge that he had endogenous depression that was likely to recur throughout his lifetime. Apparently there was to be no stopping the autonomous neurochemical incidents that littered his history and threatened his future. He was advised that the quality of his life would be improved by learning to manage his illness.

Over the years he had learned to live with what he considered to be an inherent disability rather than something for which he was personally liable. In being able to name his enemy he was able to move away from the terrors of the unknown and now saw his bouts of depression as unsocial calls from a familiar, though unwelcome, visitor. The resultant slide into a world of harrowing bleakness was still terrifying, but he realised was temporary. Beyond the realisation (hope?) that the periods of illness were short-lived, lay the bleaker prospect of 'what if'. What if several 'incidents' followed each other quickly, before he had time to recover? Would the bleakness become a permanent feature? Would he fall over the edge into the darkness from which none escape? In spite of his mood, Sludge could not resist a wry smile at the irony that such thoughts in themselves were depressing.

As he learned about his illness he also learned to recognise his own tendency to wallow in an aura of comfortable melancholy. Still sitting on the floor he welcomed the self-diagnosis that he was not (at that moment anyway) clinically depressed, he was merely melancholic and so allowed himself to luxuriate in that feeling, conjuring memories of his dead parents to feed the mood. In one of his short stories, John Steinbeck had referred to Sludge's sought-for state of mind as 'emotional saturation'; Sludge couldn't recall which story.

Walking across to the bookcase he took down a comb-bound manuscript. Written on the front cover in pen was the title, *Travels of a Cold Eyed Man* by Tex Ace. Sludge's father, Les Ludgeworth, was a writer for D C Thomson of Dundee, publishers of comic books for boys. As Les Ludge he wrote for the *Wizard*, mainly football stories featuring Bruddersford Town and their perennial battles either for promotion, or against relegation. Les introduced his older son Eddie into the team as Flying Eddie Ludgeworth, the winged winger with magic in his boots whose goals took them to an FA Cup Final. Although kidnapped on the eve of the Final, Flying Eddie managed to escape and got to the ground in time to play the last five minutes and to score the two goals needed to take the cup back to an ecstatic Bruddersford.

Sludge had never made it into the comic books due to the fact that a particularly odious villain in one of his father's stories turned out to have the same name as, and close resemblance to, a senior executive manager employed by his publisher, although no one noticed until the story had been published. By a piece of unfortunate timing the resulting kerfuffle in his publishers boardroom coincided with the time that his contract was up for renewal. Before Les had been able find a suitable fictional persona for his youngest child he found himself unemployed. Another unfortunate piece of timing found Les out of work at a time when the market for his type of prose story was rapidly diminishing.

With time on his hands, and to help his son through his periods of illness, Les created the character of Young Billy Ludgeworth also known as the Durango Kid. He told his son countless stories about how Durango was a nerveless, cold-eyed man who roamed the ranges of the Wild West, fighting injustice and righting wrongs wherever he found them. In response to his son's request for a companion (a side kick, Billy had said, rather self-consciously), Les introduced into the stories an older man called Tex Ace who, in habits and appearance bore a striking similarity to Les himself. Sludge's plans, when he was in America, to visit the town of Durango and the other haunts of Young Billy Ludgeworth, were thwarted by his expulsion, and that was a constant source of regret.

Sludge had never known that the stories were written down until his father died and he found a batch of forty-two copied out in his father's neat hand. After adding a title page Sludge had had the stories bound and still toyed with the vague idea that he might have them typed so as to send them to a publisher sometime. In fact, a publisher's agent had looked informally at the handwritten manuscript and suggested that, with some input from Sludge, 'something could be done'. That was a few years ago and Sludge was still thinking about it. Placing the manuscript on the table he flicked through the pages until he came to *The Durango Kid and Tex in Uncharted Territory*, sitting down he began to read.

'Damn!' he said as the buzzer on his wall announced that he had a visitor. 'Double damn!' he said, remembering that the intercom was broken and that he would have to walk down three flights of stairs to answer the door.

'This is yours I believe Dr Ludgeworth?'

On opening the door Sludge was greeted by a tall young man wearing a green Barbour jacket. He noted with some surprise that the man was holding the wine glass he had thrown from the window and that it appeared to be undamaged.

The cold-eyed man regarded the stranger coolly and noted that his smiling mouth disagreed with the rest of his expression.

'Thank you.' Sludge said, taking the glass from the young man with no more apparent reaction than it was an everyday occurrence that someone should retrieve a wine glass from his garden having first seen it thrown from an upstairs window.

'Was there something else?' he asked as the young man, having given up the glass, showed no signs of withdrawing.

'Yes, there is.' said the young man, 'I would like to talk to you for a few minutes; if that is at all possible.' he smiled.

'Talk about what?'

'About you and Mr Bleaney and his diaries.' said the young man.

The cold-eyed man sensed danger. This was no ordinary stranger. He had a presence that oozed menace. The cold-eyed man opted for the long game.

'I can talk to you about Albert Bleaney,' said Sludge, 'but I know nothing about any diaries.' Stepping to one side, he held the door open. 'Would you like to come in,' he invited the young man, 'I can probably find something to put in this glass,' he held up the rescued item, 'while I tell you what little I know.'

Walking from the kitchen with two glasses, Sludge saw his guest was glancing at the open manuscript lying on the table.

'I don't suppose this is Mr Bleaney's work?' he asked.

'Hardly,' Sludge said, 'to the best of my knowledge he never wrote cowboy stories. No,' he continued, amused at the other's mistake, 'they were written by my father many years ago.'

'Your father is Tex Ace?'

'Was.' said Sludge, 'Long story.' He handed the young man a glass and indicated he should take a seat at the table. 'More to the point. Who are you, and what is your story?'

Realising that he could not pass himself off as being knowledgeable about the poet's work, the young man, adopting a straightforward and businesslike manner, said,

'My name is Barbour. I am acting for someone who has a very great interest in Mr Bleaney's diaries. Can you help me to locate them?'

The cold-eyed man felt a charge of tension in the air. Drawing deeply on his cigarette he thought about the proposition. Exhaling slowly, he watched the smoke drift lazily upward until, caught by a draught, it suddenly swirled and swerved through the open window. He had seen these fresh-faced kids before, all innocent questions one minute and blazing forty-fives the next, just because they didn't like the answers.

Reflecting on the unusual experience of being presented with two hidden identities within a few hours, Sludge smiled inwardly at the audacity of the obviously assumed name, 'He could have picked Gewurztraminer,' he thought looking at the bottle of wine on the table, 'now that would have been challenging'.

He shrugged, 'I've already told you. I don't know anything about any diaries.' Holding the bottle up to the light to see how much was left, 'Enough for half a glass each.' he said. 'Anyway, who do you represent? What are you? Publisher? Free-lance? Newspaper man?' Sludge didn't know why he didn't expect the truth from the young man; perhaps twenty odd years of dealing with students and their peculiarly mendacious ways had taught him something after all he thought. He poured the wine, taking care to apportion equal amounts.

The young man stared at the wine glass as if uncertain of something. His Barbour coat was hanging open and both hands were thrust deep into the pockets. He was sitting perfectly still. Standing at the head of the table Sludge observed that Mr Barbour was wearing well cut moleskin trousers, dark brown with a raised side seam, tan desert boots, and his shirt, open at the neck, was pale cream with a subtle brown and red check. 'Home counties, upper middle class, self confident.' he thought.

The cold-eyed man knew this was the moment. He had faced this so often. If the young man was going to draw his gun it would happen in the next few seconds. Breathing slowly and regularly the cold-eyed man relaxed, and waited.

'Dr Ludgeworth,' the young man sighed, 'I have no doubt that Bleaney told you about mysterious visitors and their questions about matters of national security. I have no doubt that he kept a diary. I also have no doubt that the drunken old fool who survived him knew nothing, but you,' he lifted his gaze from the wine glass and stared at Sludge, 'I am not so sure. Not so sure at all. What do you know Dr Ludgeworth? Have you found the diaries? Have you found anything,' he paused, 'unusual?' Resting his hand on the table he placed his thumb and forefinger around the stem of the wine glass and began to twist it gently from side to side while holding his unblinking stare on Sludge. 'Anything unusual, of, how shall we say, a very personal nature, intimate even?'

Sludge had the teacher's gift of being able to hold a reasonable discussion on one topic while at the same time his brain was engaged on a different topic. So it was that, although his mind was dealing with the possible equation of 'unusual' + 'personal' + 'intimate' = 'pubic hair', he could smile in the face of the other's unflinching gaze, and reply, 'We only took possession of the house very recently. A great deal of work has to be done before we can be sure of what is, and what isn't, there. Of course the house has many things that could be described as 'unusual' and 'personal'. Can you be more specific?'

'That isn't necessary.' said Barbour standing up, his wine untouched. 'When you find it you will know. Then you will tell me. About that, and the diaries.' Sludge could feel the other's breath on his face as the young man moved to stand close to him. The young man spoke softly, 'You will tell me, won't you Dr Ludgeworth?' Without waiting for a reply he walked to the door, with his hand on the doorknob he turned, 'Not to tell me would be very silly,' he said, his voice suddenly harsh and threatening, 'very silly indeed.' Then he left the room; Sludge heard him descending the stairs and the front door slam shut. From his dormer window Sludge watched the young man in the green Barbour jacket stride purposefully across the road to disappear into the shadow of the trees.

From his vantage point the cold-eyed man flicked the butt of his Marlboro up into the air and waited for the burst of sparks as it landed. 'That sure is one mean son-of-a-gun.' he murmured to himself as he looked at the dark blue profile of the mesquite trees outlined against the night sky.

'Dear God, Albert,' Sludge addressed the empty room, 'what was that all about?' Reaching into the inside pocket of the jacket hanging on the back of the chair recently occupied by the young man in the Barbour he removed a long manila wallet. From the wallet he took out a small transparent envelope containing some, as yet unidentified, flower petals and a curl, also unidentified, of pubic hair. 'He was right,' he said looking at the envelope, 'I have found it and I do know. This must be the 'unusual' and 'personal' item. But why is it so important? How can this be a matter of national security? What the hell did you get up to, Albert?'

Sludge opened another bottle of wine, poured himself a glass and sat down to consider his options. Of one thing he was sure. Whatever else he did, he would delay his agreement to destroy the contents of the envelope until he knew a little more. He also decided that he would tell Joan and the others that the packet had been destroyed.

It was a tired and confused man that eventually went to bed having decided nothing else other than, as he was banned from going to the University, he would call into 105 West Bank in the morning and have a 'good root about'. His car was still unusable and he considered contacting Beryl or Joan to cadge a lift, but after some thought he decided to go alone. He felt sure that if he did find the diaries, the fewer people that knew the better it would be.

The Crow Dream

The visit from Mr Barbour had disturbed Sludge. He slept fitfully, partly because he had drunk enough wine to experience the rapid whirling plummet every time he closed his eyes, partly because his injured tongue hurt, but mainly because he was worried. Around three o'clock in the morning it occurred to him that Albert Bleaney had been a spy.

Some five hours later Sludge dismissed his early hours revelation as absurd. 'What is it about three o'clock?' he muttered to himself while gloomily examining an almost empty cereal packet. This time it had brought him nonsense, but three a.m. could bring him visits of overwhelming dread when his body would shake with an unnamed terror. A terror that didn't vanish with the morning, but faded to a shadow that was to remain on the edge of his vision for days afterwards. Sludge shuddered at the memory. 'Pull yourself together man,' he said, with a mocking smile at the uselessness of such advice.

Although Sludge was certain that Albert Bleaney had not been a spy it was clear that he had done something, or become involved in something, that had attracted the attention of the security services, whoever they were. That they remained interested after his death indicated that he had, or they thought he had, possessed something they wanted. Whatever it was, it was apparent that they also suspected he had recorded the event in his diary. 'What happened when you went to the Palace, Albert?' Sludge said to himself as he turned the small plastic envelope over and over in his fingers.

On the reasonable assumption, rather than paranoid, he assured himself, that the front of the house might well be under observation, Sludge decided to leave via the back garden on his way to 105 West Bank. The house had a long rear garden that had once backed onto a railway line, now converted into a cycling track that ran from the city centre almost out to the coast. At one point the track ran fairly close to West Bank; Sludge knew that sometimes Albert Bleaney had taken that route when he came to see him. Sludge still owned Mr Bleaney's bike, in fact he was proud that he had kept it in rideable condition. Sitting on the bicycle now with one foot on a pedal, the toes of the other foot on the ground and with his Stetson hat hooked onto a handlebar, he reached into his top pocket and took out a pair of sunglasses that he put on with a flourish. Placing his hat squarely on his head he said loudly with a North American nasal twang, 'It's night time, we're wearing sunglasses and it's a hundred miles to Chicago.'

Standing up on the pedals and transferring his weight from side to side he began to pick up speed pedalling along the track, happy at the thought that the bicycle was heading for its ancestral home.

The cold-eyed man glanced at the trees bordering the trail. Whoever was out there couldn't see him and, 'I can't see them,' he thought grimly. He was on a mission. Not a mission from God, but a mission nonetheless. The enemy was unknown; the goal uncertain, but at stake was the reputation of his friend. His good friend. He must not fail. Pausing at a crossing place the cold-eyed man scrutinised the area carefully, 'Good place for an ambush.' he recognised. Satisfied that it was safe to cross, looking to the left and right, he walked his steed through before remounting and riding on. Reaching a high point above West Bank the cold-eyed man stopped and looked down through the trees. He could see 105; it looked deserted. There was a postman going from house to house.

With a shout of, 'Wagons roll!' and his coat streaming behind him Sludge freewheeled down the railway embankment. His feet off the pedals and toes pointing to the sky, he held his legs out stiffly as he burst through a small hedge and bumped out onto the small lane that ran at the back of the houses on East Bank. Pedalling hard he followed the curving lane to its junction with West Bank where he swerved quickly to his right for a few yards then veered left into the driveway of number 105. Unlocking the door quickly he propped his bicycle in the hallway before turning to drop the latch, and to make certain that the door was securely fastened.

The cold-eyed man stood perfectly still. He fought against the dangerous feeling of exhilaration. He had reached his destination safely, but he knew that the journey was just beginning. He breathed deeply and slowly to bring his heart rate under control, then, moving stealthily, he entered a book-lined room. Standing well back from the window the cold-eyed man looked out. He was pleased with what he saw. West Bank was quiet, even the postman had gone. He stood there for several minutes, waiting, watching. Nothing happened.

Sludge was tired; he felt the exhilaration of the cycle ride drain from him. His change of mood was tangible. As one mood departed he felt another slide in to take its place. The reality of his situation pressed on him; he was suspended and very likely to lose his job. Peter Pelham would continue to prosper, and there was the lurking threat from the menacing Mr Barbour.

Sludge had never liked this house. The only room he had ever felt comfortable in was a small room upstairs at the back of the house that had a small balcony overlooking the rambling garden. He looked into the room and remembered how on summer evenings he and Albert would sit in the two leather armchairs that dominated the room, more so now that they were covered in dustsheets. Here they would share a six-pack of Guinness and watch the changing patterns in the sky while listening to *Blonde on Blonde*, *Blood on the Tracks*, or more likely, *Bringing it all Back Home*. Together they never listened to anyone other than Bob Dylan because Albert loved to hear, 'One of the finest poets of the twentieth century strutting his stuff'.

It was in this room, thought Sludge looking about him, that after showing a composed face for his parents he had broken down completely when telling Albert that his brother Eddie had died. Less than two years later Les Ludgeworth died, unable to come to terms with the death of his eldest son. To Sludge's horror his father appeared to simply fade away, and then vanish. The deaths of his father and brother disconnected Sludge to an extent that Sheila, his partner, couldn't bear, and she left for Aarhus. Not only in the hope that Sludge would eventually follow her, but also to keep a grip on her own sense of self. Two years after Sheila had left, Sludge's mother died. When Albert Bleaney, who had become his friend and confidant died just one year later, Sludge had to reconcile his avowedly solitary nature with the fact that contrary to what he suspected was a widely held view, he was a lonely man. Five years had passed and Sludge was still struggling to find a sense of purpose that had largely been missing since he was forced to leave America.

'It was a bad time for the kid.' the cold-eyed man drawled. 'All his kinfolk dead and his woman gone.' He drew heavily on his cigarette. 'It was a very bad time.' Squinting through the smoke at the figure in the armchair he slowly shook his head. 'And it isn't over yet.' he said.

Sludge was asleep. He dreamed that he was a crow. He was a very large black crow standing in the top of an oak tree that was pitching gently like a galleon in full sail on a rolling sea. From between his feet he could see down through the twisted confusion of branches to the ground below. As the tree moved so his field of vision shifted. He could see a man was standing at the bottom of the tree, sometimes he could see his upturned face then the tree would move and he would lose sight of it until the tree moved again. He saw the man begin to climb. He was climbing very quickly.

A sense of fear drove the crow to launch his heavy body from the treetop perch, experiencing as he did so a delicious moment of panic as his weight pulled him downwards in a ponderous fall before the powerful muscles in his wings took over and lifted him slowly upward in a wide soaring arc. He was very high when he turned to see that the man had reached the top of the tree and was waving up at him. The crow began a gradual spiralling descent to get close enough to see the man's face, but remaining out of reach of him.

Sludge knew the man was his father. He could see his lips were moving and that he appeared to be saying something. The crow strained to hear, but was too far away. The man beckoned him closer, but the crow stayed out of reach. He could feel his wings getting heavier and more difficult to move as the man disappeared beneath the treetop canopy of leaves. As he hung uncomfortably in the air he saw the leaves on the tree begin to shrivel and turn black.

SEVEN

The Message in Snowden's Entrails

Sludge woke up with a start. 'My God,' he said, 'I must have been asleep for hours, it's getting dark'. After looking at his watch and taking off his sunglasses, he realised that it was only mid morning. The dream lingered with him. A black crow laboured low across the skyline and he felt its heaviness as it lifted itself to land on a rooftop television aerial that swayed under its weight.

'Come on,' he said, smacking his hands together, 'let's get this show on the road.' After some thought he decided that the best strategy was to walk through the house slowly. He would start in the hall and look in each room in turn. The plan was to stand in the middle of each room just looking around to see if anything 'jumped out at him'. If that failed then he would have to wait until the Committee members came down to make a detailed inventory of the entire contents of the house. Barbour's interest apart, Sludge wanted to get his hands on the diary before Ronan 'Scoop' Coyne, otherwise anything could happen in the joint names of publicity and career advancement. Joan was organising the inventory and, as far as he was aware, it was due to take place sometime next Wednesday. No doubt she would be at the walk tomorrow and would give him the details then.

Sludge hurried down the stairs. He paused, listening to the approach of a car; it passed the house and continued along West Bank. The only item in the hall was his bicycle and a small side table littered with unopened circulars and letters from Reader's Digest that he felt he could safely ignore. 'I wonder if Molly was right about the house having been searched,' he mused as he walked into the living room cum study, 'if that is so, if the house has already been searched by professionals, am I likely to find anything?'

The alcoves on either side of the fireplace had been fitted with shelves that were crammed with books. Above the fireplace a mantelshelf held a clock and a pair of china King Charles spaniels that Sludge knew had belonged to Albert's grandmother. A bay window gave a view onto West Bank with a small desk occupying the bay; on either side of the desk were bookcases, also full. The wall opposite the window held a large glass fronted bureau, full of books.

'Must be well over a thousand in here alone', said Sludge to himself, knowing that this room held only a small percentage of the total number of books in the house. 'It's going to be one hell of an inventory Joan,' he smiled walking slowly about the room, 'how are your library skills?'

Suddenly, with a visual version of that phenomenon of selective perception that allows people to hear their name mentioned on the other side of a crowded and noisy room, Sludge saw a copy of the book he had written nearly twenty years ago. Opening the glass doors of the bureau he read the title, *An Unsettled Spirit*, and underneath that, William S Ludgeworth. Sludge had been unaware that Albert had a copy of his book and was overwhelmed by the realisation that his friend had taken the trouble to obtain what was, he admitted, a book of limited appeal. The book in his hand, Sludge read, for the first time in many years, the quotation from the Zimbabwean writer Dambudzo Marechera, that had so inspired him. He read: 'Listen, that's the song that will

forever blow like an unsettled spirit from the Zambezi –
through Harare, Bulawayo, Mutare, Gweru, down the
Limpopo and back again to the Zambezi – from which it
will again turn restlessly back searching for you and me
so that again and again we can retell their story, which is
not our story. Listen to it. How sad, how profound, and
yet so heartbreakingly pitiful.'

With a deep sigh, perhaps for a lost world and a lost
opportunity, or for an ambition that had withered, he
turned the page. To his amazement, he saw a short note
addressed to him. It read, 'Hi Billy, Remember Saturday
lunchtimes with Harry?' It was initialled 'AB'. Beneath
that appeared the piece from Subterranean Homesick
Blues, obviously copied out by Albert Bleaney.

The m**a**n in the t**r**ench coat
Badge out, l**a**id off
Says he's got a ba**d** cou**gh**
Wants to g**e**t it paid off
Look out kid
It's **s**omethi**n**' I did

As he had now met the menacing Mr Barbour the
warning implicit in the last two lines became clear. It was
also clear that Albert's alteration of 'somethin' you did' to
'somethin' I did' was intentional, maybe even
confessional.

For the second time in less than twenty-four hours,
Sludge was dumbfounded by the mysterious activities of
his late friend. 'Jesus, Albert,' he gasped, 'what the hell
did you do?' He sat down at the desk, and placing the
book in front of him; he stared at the inscription. Albert
Bleaney was not a troublemaker, he was not involved in
politics, apart from declining an informal enquiry into his
interest in the Poet Laureateship, his life had been free of

controversy. Even his 'four women' had been seen as an acceptable eccentricity, the 'sort of things that poets do.' His head supported on his hands, Sludge looked at the familiar writing, willing the words to speak to him.

On looking closely he noticed that some of the letters had been outlined with a darker pen and a small line drawn under them. Taking a pen from his inside jacket pocket he transcribed the letters onto a scrap of paper he found on the desk. He looked at the letters and read them out slowly, 'a, r, b, a, d, h, e, l, s, n, makes arbadhelsn?' he said, 'which is absolute nonsense. What game are you playing Albert?'

Deep in thought he lifted his head and was aghast to find he was looking into the unsmiling face of Mr Barbour who was standing in the front garden very close to the window. The young man gazed at Sludge for a few seconds then pointed to his right towards the front door and making a turning motion with his right hand he signalled he wanted to enter the house. Completely taken aback, all Sludge could do was to nod weakly and head for the door.

The cold-eyed man was furious. He had been stupid. He had been outwitted. He had allowed himself to be sidetracked. His enemy was clever. He must by all accounts keep cool now and keep a clear head. All could be won or lost in the next few minutes. Standing in the cold hallway he unbuckled his guns and placed them on a small side table. It was important that the other should think he presented no danger. The cold-eyed man composed himself. A short, impatient knocking signalled the mood of the unwelcome visitor. Counting slowly to ten the cold-eyed man smiled a thin smile and waited.

Sludge opened the door. 'Found another wineglass Mr Barbour?' he said.

'More to the point, Dr Ludgeworth, what have you found?' said the tall young man as he pushed past Sludge and entered the house. 'Anything of interest?' he said going into the study and approaching the desk where he picked up Sludge's book.

'Only if you are interested in the literature of central Southern Africa.' said Sludge. Realising that he had the scrap of paper in his hand, and that it might raise questions he couldn't answer, he screwed it into a ball and slipped it into his pocket while Mr Barbour flicked through the pages of *An Unsettled Spirit*.

'So, you are a writer as well.' said the young man looking at the front cover, 'I take it that this William S Ludgeworth and you, are one and the same?'

'Yes.'

Barbour looked up sharply at the terseness and non-elaborative nature of the reply and dropped the book onto the desk. 'O.K.' he said. 'Let's cut to the chase. What decisions have you come to following our conversation of last night?'

'Decisions,' said Sludge, 'what's to decide? You're searching for something that is in some way so special that you can't, or won't, tell me what it is, other than if I find it, I will know. If, and until, I do find whatever-it-is, there is no decision to be made.' He shrugged his shoulders. 'You, or whoever you represent, want the diaries. I don't believe that there are any diaries. Again, I have no decision to make.'

The cold-eyed man watched the man in the Barbour jacket carefully. He was going to raise the stakes. He changed his position so that the window was behind him; he could see Barbour's face clearly while his own face was in shadow.

'Surely,' said Sludge, 'if there was anything to be found, you would have found it by now. This house has been searched often enough.'

'Ah, so you do know about that.' said Mr Barbour, lifting his eyebrows in a quizzical, half mocking fashion. 'What else do you know?' He moved to sit in one of the armchairs flanking the fireplace and indicating its companion opposite, said, 'Sit down, Dr Ludgeworth, let's talk about this.'

Sludge remained standing. He needed time. Time to decipher the code, if that is what it was. Time to discover the significance of the contents of the envelope. Albert had left a message for him; he needed time to discover the exact nature of that message before he gave any information at all to Mr Barbour.

'Dr Ludgeworth,' the young man broke into the silence, his elbows on the arms of the chair and his steepled fingers beneath his chin, 'do not get any further involved. Tell me what you know, and walk away.' His tone was soft, pleading almost.

The cold-eyed man was impressed by the young man's changed demeanour. He was a professional. His offer was very tempting. It was too late for the kid to claim that the package had been found and destroyed, but it could be surrendered. No one would be any the wiser. If that happened he could ride away without a backward glance. He knew that that, however tempting, wouldn't happen. He had never left a job unfinished and he was too old to start now. He would see this one through to the end, whatever the cost.

'Mr Barbour,' said Sludge with as much resolve as he could muster against the self assurance of the athletic young man, 'you were not invited into this house and I must ask you to leave immediately. I told you last night and I confirm it now. I have nothing, and I know nothing. Further discussion would be pointless. Please leave.'

'Bad call,' said Mr Barbour coldly, 'a very bad call.'

He continued to sit in the armchair, his steepled fingers now touching his nose, his thumbs hooked under his chin; his eyes closed, he looked as if he was praying. Suddenly he stood up, 'When I was a child,' he said picking up one of the china spaniels from the mantelshelf, 'I saw a very bad film in which the villains tried to frighten someone by breaking a few cheap baubles.' He dropped the figure onto the hearth where it shattered. 'I don't think it worked, it seemed to me to be overly melodramatic, and not very effective.' He picked up the remaining ornament, 'I thought then, and experience has proved me right, that people are more frightened by personal invasion, by physical pain,' he dropped the second dog onto the hearth, 'than by the mindless destruction of inanimate objects. What do you think, Dr Ludgeworth? What frightens you more, the sight of these fragments,' without taking his eyes off Sludge he crushed some of the broken pieces under his boot, 'or the thought that you might be subjected to physical pain? What frightens you?'

The cold-eyed man was glad he'd left his guns in the hall. This was not the time for heroics. Holding his jacket open with his left hand to show that he was unarmed he used the finger and thumb of his right hand to extract his packet of Marlboros from his breast pocket. Shaking a cigarette halfway out of the pack he took it in his teeth and replaced the pack before slowly and carefully he retrieved a match from the same pocket. Holding the match in the crook of his forefinger, he flicked it into flame with his thumbnail and lit his cigarette. He blew out the flame with a stream of smoke before tossing the spent match into the hearth among the remnants of the china dogs.

Though shocked by the sudden violence, Sludge was not frightened. He sensed that he could move the exchange onto ground more familiar to him, as dealing with philosophical questions was his stock-in-trade. 'What frightens me?' said Sludge, 'Not this,' he pointed at the hearth, 'not you. I have no doubt that you are capable of inflicting pain, but no,' he shook his head, 'that doesn't frighten me.'

Because he was unsure that his legs were able to keep him upright, he moved to sit opposite the man, who remained standing. 'I will tell you what frightens me. Have you read *Catch 22*, the novel by Joseph Heller?' He enquired in a conversational tone that took the young man completely by surprise. 'No? What do you read - no, let me guess.' He held up his hand to stop the other from replying, although Mr Barbour had shown no inclination to do so. 'You read *Horse and Hounds* for light relief, and the *Lives of the Great Leaders* for intellectual stimulation. Wait, wait,' he said, as the young man showed signs of irritation, 'I haven't answered your question yet.'

'Yossarian is the hero; some might say anti-hero of the novel.' Sludge continued. 'He is a member of a bomber crew based on a fictional island, fighting a bloody war. On one flight the airplane is hit by flak, and a crewman, Bombardier Snowden, is wounded in the thigh. Yossarian, although squeamish, attends to the wound, which gets increasingly gory as the novel progresses. His apparently successful ministrations to the wounded crewman, as the airplane heads back to base, are explored in linear, though episodic form, throughout the novel as Yossarian's story unfolds. Are you with me so far?' He smiled at the young man. 'I'll take that as a yes.' he said in response to the silence and the accompanying hostile glare.

'Eventually, as they approach home and safety, Yossarian discovers he has been treating a superficial wound, unaware that Snowden has received a mortal wound to the chest. When he does notice the wound and moves Snowden's jacket, the bombardier's guts spill out onto the floor. Snowden is not yet dead, but, according to Yossarian, it was easy to read the message in the entrails spread out in front of him. Of course,' he went on in his best seminar manner, 'not all critics agree on the nature of the message in Snowden's entrails.'

'Here is a possible interpretation. Yossarian had tended to the man's wounds to the best of his ability, but he had missed the major trauma, the wound that actually killed him. He had continued, in blissful ignorance, with his plasters and bandages, but he was unaware of the existence of the wound that was to cause death. So, it is implied in the novel, or could be so implied, that Yossarian had lived his life more or less successfully; he had dealt with the minutiae, the trivia of day to day existence, unaware that he was, in effect, bleeding to death and all because of ignorance, of carelessness. That is what frightens me.'

Sludge eased himself out of the chair and walked across to the desk to pick up his book. 'That is what really frightens me,' he faced the young man, 'the possibility that I am living my life believing that I am doing O.K. But that something that is close to me, and is quite literally dreadful, exists unknown to me. Something, that if I did know about, I may be able to resolve. But as I am ignorant, and possibly careless in my unknowing, I am doing nothing, and so one day, this something will become known to me, and will cause me such pain, such revision, that it will nullify everything I have done in my life.'

'Impressive', said the young man walking to the door, 'very impressive, but absolute bullshit. When you return to the real world,' he said, 'I'll be here, waiting for you.'

Thoughtfully, and with no little apprehension, Sludge watched Mr Barbour leave. Maybe the menacing young man was right, maybe he had talked bullshit. Perhaps that is what I do, Sludge thought unhappily, I offer pseudo-intellectual comments while misquoting half remembered texts and personalising issues, to make it appear that I have deeply held convictions.

He had not told the truth. Mr Barbour did frighten him. Not in the same way, that facing the National Guard in Dallas, Texas, more than twenty years ago had frightened him. Then it had been the unreasoning hatred in the eyes of the part-time soldiers, the realisation that they wanted to hurt people, simply because they were trained to do just that and here was an opportunity. They probably did hate students he reflected, but it could have been any section of society: strikers, immigrants, the disadvantaged, as long as for a while, and for whatever reason, they were designated as 'enemies of the state', then violence could legitimately be used in subduing them. Sludge faced the National Guard because he held the same beliefs as the students. The relationship was not one of academic and students, it was one of a purpose shared by a group of committed men and women. He didn't set out to confront the redneck militia, but when it came to doing just that, he didn't back away.

Mr Barbour was different. There was no passion in his violence. It was a means to an end, no more, no less. If it was expedient to break bones, then he would break bones, Sludge was quite certain. He could imagine him saying, 'Nothing personal old man. It's just a matter of business.' as he slipped a long slim blade expertly between the fourth and fifth rib. The complete lack of emotion and the dedication to the job in hand that Sludge sensed in the essentially amoral young man, he found truly frightening. Just as frightening was the fact that he had deliberately conveyed his threatening message in two very short encounters. Sludge anticipated that the third meeting was likely to see an escalation of action as Mr Barbour sought a solution to his problem. In spite of this, until Sludge had a clear idea of what was involved, he had no intention of cooperating with him.

The cold-eyed man picked up his guns and refastened them. He knew that the poet, the old timer, had helped the kid when his world began to fall apart. Nothing fancy, he'd just been there. He sucked deeply on his cigarette. There were times when the old guy had gently nudged Sludge from riding the wrong trail. He had looked for answers in the darkness, but the old timer had pointed his face to the dawn. Yep, he owed him. No doubt about that. The cold-eyed man sat back in the chair and tipping his hat over his eyes, he feigned sleep and waited.

Subterranean Homesick Blues

As he realised that the gnawing feeling in the pit of his stomach was as much due to the absence of breakfast as to the presence of fear, Sludge decided to cycle the mile or so to the Brickies. There he could eat an awful pie, have a pint of stout to settle his nerves, and take time to consider the conundrum left to him by Mr Bleaney.

Harry Cooper was stacking empties in the yard at the rear of his public house when Sludge cycled round the corner. 'Morning Billy,' he said, 'I hope you haven't come to spit on my windows.'

A large man, now in his late sixties, Harry had been a professional rugby league player. He had in fact represented Great Britain, before he became a publican, and he still had the sense of humour he claimed was a prerequisite for playing the toughest contact sport in the world. 'Put your bike in there,' he pointed to a storeroom, 'it'll be safe from the thieving students that hang around here.' he laughed. 'Mind you,' he added in mock serious tones, 'at least they don't vomit blood and Guinness all over the place.'

Sludge had dismounted and was standing next to his bicycle holding the handlebars. He liked Harry Cooper, but was often dumbfounded by his relentless barrage of bonhomie. 'I'm sorry - ' he began only to be interrupted as the landlord took the bicycle from his hands and placed it in the store, behind some crates.

'Now,' Harry said, as he emerged, 'we don't usually see you this early, have you come for an awful pie?' One of Albert Bleaney's most anthologised poems was *Mockery's Mother*, which features the poet returning from his less-than-inspiring involvement in a badly organised CND Rally in Rotherham. According to the poem, on his way home he called into a public house and ate 'an awful pie'. He was later to claim that he ate the pie in Brickies, (he didn't, it was in Goole), but ever since then Harry Cooper had included on his bar lunch menu an 'awful pie', that was actually a very tasty meat and potato concoction.

'Come on,' he said, placing an arm affectionately around Sludge's shoulders, 'let's see what we can find.' Because of his background in rugby league Harry was a team player. He didn't understand the university lecturers who figured among his customers, they were amiable enough, not standoffish at all, but in spite of their education and their strings of qualifications, it seemed to him that not many of them knew how to make friends. He considered them to be an odd collection of individuals with no sense of shared purpose that he could see. Sludge he thought was a 'lovely man' who could be very amusing, but he had an air of vulnerability about him that puzzled Harry who had the mistaken impression that higher education brought with it self-assurance and self-determination.

A few minutes later Sludge was sitting in a secluded part of the saloon bar, his book was on the table. 'The window cleaned up nicely.' He nodded across the room as Harry placed a large plate of pie and chips in front of him.

'Try to get outside if you fancy a repeat performance.' Harry responded with a wry smile. 'Can I get you anything else?' He stood silently for a moment before adding, 'I've heard about your suspension Billy, if there is anything I can do, you have only to ask.'

Touched by his obvious sincerity and solicitude, Sludge said, 'That's a generous offer Harry, at the moment there is nothing. If there is, I will certainly take you up on that.' Both men stood in silence for a few moments, then as Harry was about to walk away, Sludge smiled, 'Actually there is something, it's nothing to do with the university.' he said, 'take a look at this.' He pushed his book across the table, open at Albert Bleaney's inscription. 'What do you make of it?' he said.

Harry looked at the book for a few seconds before lifting his gaze to look at Sludge. He lowered his eyes and read in a surprisingly soft voice, 'Hi Billy, Remember Saturday lunchtimes with Harry? AB. AB is Albert Bleaney I take it, although I don't recognise the poem,' he said, 'it isn't one of his, is it?' What does the reference to Saturday lunchtimes mean?'

'Yes,' Sludge said, 'the message, such as it is, is from Albert and, no, the poem isn't one of his. Saturday lunchtimes? I was hoping that you could tell me.'

'Why are some of the letters picked out?'

'So far that's another mystery. I copied them out, I've got it here somewhere.' He searched his pockets until he retrieved the screwed up piece of paper. Smoothing it out on the table, he showed the result to Harry.

'Arbadhelsn,' said Harry, who had taken a seat opposite Sludge and was now frowning at the piece of paper, 'arbadhelsn,' he repeated, this time emphasising the third syllable rather that the second, 'however you say it, it still makes no bleeding sense. Is it some sort of daft joke?'

Sludge shook his head. 'Definitely not a joke.'

'You see what you can do with your awful pie,' said Harry, standing up, 'and while you are doing that I'll put the old grey matter to work. Arbadhelsn,' he muttered, absent-mindedly flicking a bar towel back and forth as he walked away.

He returned a few minutes later with a broad smile on his face. 'Cracked it Billy.' he said, sitting down, 'Every Saturday I do the crossword in the Independent, I have done for years.' he said. 'I remember that you and Albert used to meet here regularly on Saturday lunchtime, and if I was stuck for answers, you would help me out. I reckon that his note in your book refers to that. As I remember, you, Billy, were particularly good at anagrams.' Frowning, he lifted a chip off Sludge's plate and considered it carefully before placing it in his mouth, 'Home made these, you know. You won't get ready-made stuff here.' he said with the authority of a connoisseur. Looking again at the scrap of paper on which Sludge had written out the letters, he read out, 'a,r,b,a,d,h,e,l,s,n. Albert's left you a puzzle to solve. I reckon these letters,' he tapped the paper, 'are an anagram.'

Sludge, who hadn't risked a response as he had a mouthful of pie, swallowed and nodded, 'Could be, Harry, could be.'

'O.K. I'm coming.' Harry signalled across to the bar. 'Duty calls, Billy. If you need any more help don't hesitate to ask.' he said, laughing as he walked across to attend to his customers. 'Now then gents, what can I get you?'

Sludge recognised the two men as distant colleagues. They had been at the university for almost as long as he had, but they worked in a different department and, although they taught the same students and sometimes worked on the same degree courses as he did, the relationship had remained entirely formal. He had often wondered why it was that no social life appeared to exist in the university. Was it because all his colleagues were self-sufficient? Or did his own tendency to plough a lonely furrow cause such activities to be concealed from him? He raised his hand in acknowledgement of their waved greeting and watched as they headed for the other side of the large room. In his head he heard Sheila's cheery call of, 'Come on over here and join us, why don't you?', but he knew that such gestures were beyond him.

The cold-eyed man avoided friends. In his line of work, they could be a liability. He had places to go, things to do. He must be ready to ride anywhere, at any time. No ties meant no farewells.

Sludge sighed and looked at the scrap of paper. It could be an anagram, he thought without enthusiasm. He rearranged the letters into a column.

ar
ba
dh
el
sn

Experience had taught him that it was easier to see alternatives when letters were written this way. He had no idea whether he was looking for one word or more, so he began to write down words made from the assorted letters. He wrote single words, 'bread', 'bland', 'share'; he used all ten letters in making 'a rash blend', and another single word in 'barhand', with the letters 'l', 'e' and 's', left unused.

'Any luck, Billy?' called Harry from the bar.

'Not unless you once employed a bar hand called les,' Sludge said, shaking his head, 'or, do you have 'bar handles' anywhere?'

''Fraid not,' said Harry, 'unless you mean these.' he indicated the beer pumps.

'This is a hopeless task, Harry,' he said, approaching the bar with his plate and empty glass. He touched his finger to the brim of his hat in salute, 'I'll be in touch.'

'Don't forget your bike, Billy.' Harry called after his friend.

A light rain had started to fall as Billy retrieved his bicycle from behind the beer crates. He stood in the shelter of the store while he fastened his jacket and turned up his coat collar as the rain became heavier. From the distance, he heard thunder roll, 'trouble in them thar hills', he drawled. The rain became a downpour so suddenly that even the short distance to the bar would have seen him drenched, and so he resigned himself to wait where he was until the storm had passed. Sitting on his bicycle with both feet on the pedals, he leaned against the wall, listening to the rhythmic drumming on the roof, and watching the angle of the falling rain change as the rain clouds swept overhead.

'John Collier, John Collier, the window to watch, John Collier.' he sang softly, remembering the television advert from the 1960s (he thought). Exactly who John Collier was and whether he sold carpets, curtains or men's suits, he couldn't remember.

'Bar handles, bar handles, I've got no idea, bar handles' he sang trying to match the jingle to the rhythm of the falling rain. 'Bar handles, bar handles,' he said 'could even be handlebars, I suppose.' Gripping the handlebars he turned the front wheel from side to side in desultory fashion, when into his head came a vision of an embarrassed solicitor pushing that very cycle towards him with the words, 'This was Mr Bleaney's bike.' Stunned by the possibility that he may have stumbled part way forward in his search for a solution, Sludge got off the cycle, propped it against the wall, and stared at it.

Several minutes later he was still staring when he realised that the rain had stopped. His options were either to go in to the bar and have another drink, go back to 105, or to return home to his flat. He had no wish to bump into Mr Barbour again. He was, in any event, too tired and dispirited to go to 105, and he was in no mood for Harry's often relentless joviality. Riding out onto the main road Sludge looked across at the university opposite, the rain had put a sheen on the ivy leaves around Carter Hall. The ivy grew very fast, thought Sludge. Several times a year he had to hack away the growth from around his window. If he was suspended for a long time then the creeper would grow unchallenged, it might even invade his room and take it over. 'I wonder if I should lock myself in while that happens,' he pondered, 'then when they finally slash their way in, all they will find will be my bones and a Stetson hat.' He laughed softly at the notion and pedalled furiously towards the park and his flat.

Sludge never knew why he twisted off the rubber handle grips to look inside the handlebars of Mr Bleaney's bike. When he reached home he took the cycle into the garden shed where it was stored, he then removed the left hand grip and looked inside it, and then in the hollow handlebar. It was empty. He repeated the exercise with the right hand grip and found a small tube had been placed in the handlebar. The tube had apparently once contained a patent medicine called Veganin, but on unscrewing the top, he found now held a small piece of tightly rolled paper. Without opening the paper, he placed it back into the tube and put the tube into his pocket. He then replaced the rubber grip on the handlebar and walked casually from the garden into the house.

Quietly he climbed the stairs and entered his flat, locking the door behind him. There were only four rooms to inspect, the living room, the bedroom, the bathroom and the kitchen. Satisfied that he was alone, he placed the tube on the table and sat looking at it. He then removed the paper and unrolled it carefully, conscious that his heart was pounding. The piece of paper was crisp with age, and crackled as he smoothed it flat. There were two numbers, one read 020 6104 8134 that he thought could be a telephone number and the other was 92/51742, which meant nothing to him at all. He turned the paper over, that side was blank.

The cold-eyed man knew that he had found the trail. The clues were there, he only needed to keep calm. He must keep going. He was on a roll.

Sludge picked up the telephone and dialled 020 6104 8134. After three rings the telephone was answered by a female voice saying, 'Good afternoon, Cuthbert, Dibble and Grubb, how may I help you?'

'Ah, yes,' said Sludge, momentarily taken aback, 'Cuthbert, Dibble and Grubb,' he said, 'What do you do?' he asked, and immediately wished he had chosen a less confrontational approach.

'What do we do?' the girl's voice sounded puzzled, 'we are solicitors.'

'Solicitors,' said Sludge, 'and, whereabouts are you?'

'Our offices are on City Wall, London,' said the girl, somewhat impatiently, 'How may I help you?'

'I've been given this telephone number, and asked to quote another number,' Sludge said realising that the exact truth would have led to questions he couldn't answer.

'What is that number, please?' said the girl.

'It's, er,' Sludge dropped the paper and scrabbled for it at his feet, 'sorry, it's 92/51742.

'92/51742, thank you. Please wait.'

Before Sludge could respond he found himself listening to Greensleeves performed, he guessed by the James Last Orchestra. He hated music used this way. What purpose did it serve, he asked himself. He also hated the tune Greensleeves itself, and was debating whether he could actually tolerate more than two verses, when the music stopped.

'Good afternoon,' said a male voice, rather fruity, and probably late middle aged thought Sludge, 'I am Charles Cuthbert. You have enquired about file 92/51742, I believe? Please tell me your name.'

There is a file? thought Sludge before he said 'Ludgeworth, William Ludgeworth.'

'One moment,' said Mr Cuthbert. Sludge could hear the sound of a keyboard. 'Would that be Dr Ludgeworth?'

'It would.' said Sludge.

'We have a package here for your collection. It has to be collected by you personally, and I must ask you to bring some form of identification, your passport, for instance. There are also some formalities to complete before I can hand the package over. It would suit me immensely to complete this business next Wednesday. Can you do that?'

Ten minutes later Sludge was standing in the bay window recess looking across the park. He had agreed an appointment with Charles Cuthbert for next Wednesday at twelve-thirty; it was to be held at the office of Cuthbert, Dibble and Grubb, City Wall, London. His absence would mean someone else would have to become involved in the inventory of 105 West Bank, but that wasn't a problem.

The cold-eyed man breathed deeply. He could feel the adrenalin rushing through him. The first shots had been fired. The action was about to start and then he would behave as he always did. He would be calm. He would be cold. He would be in charge.

In the park a tall young man wearing a green Barbour jacket looked up through the trees at the third floor window. He was watching Sludge who was absolutely motionless and had been for several minutes, apparently just staring at the trees. Shifting his position slightly without taking his eyes off his quarry the young man smiled, then turned and walked away, making sure that he remained under cover. Barbour was not sure whether or not Sludge knew anything of value or interest, but he was going on the dead poet's walk tomorrow because he felt certain that an opportunity would arise 'to move things on a bit'. 'Time for some action,' he said, rubbing his hands together, 'then I can get out of this dump'.

EIGHT

The Walk Begins

The day had started badly for Albert Bleaney Society Committee Member, Ronan Coyne, and had just got worse. When he got out of bed, he had accidentally stepped on his spectacles and broken them; he had had to repair them with a sticking plaster that was barely effective for the job. Then he cut himself several times while shaving and his face was still festooned with the pieces of paper he had used to staunch the bleeding. Now he discovered that he had been excluded from a recent, apparently very important, meeting of the Albert Bleaney Society. Ronan Coyne was a volatile man with a tendency for paranoia that he claimed to have inherited from his mother. Others (Sludge was certainly one) believed that he had taken as his central rationalising belief Philip Larkin's claim, that, 'They fuck you up / Your Mum and Dad', as a way of disowning any personal responsibility for his sometimes execrable behaviour.

It was the morning of the inaugural Albert Bleaney Walk. An event he had prepared for, and eagerly anticipated. But, just as people were beginning to gather outside St Thomas's Primary, Albert Bleaney's first school and the assembly point for the walk, Pamela had let slip that a recent meeting he had been told was cancelled, had in fact taken place. Under fiercely insistent questioning, Pamela, embarrassed and flustered by her slip, had revealed that something had been found that appeared to relate somehow to the poet's OBE, but that the committee had decided it should be 'destroyed and never mentioned again'. On recovering her composure she had told him that any questions he had should be referred to Sludge. He had decided to do just that at the first opportunity.

From his vantage position standing on the top of a small wall, Coyne looked at the thirty or so people who had gathered for the walk. At the back of the group he could see Pamela and Sludge in conversation. 'I'll take that smile off your face.' he muttered to himself, his mood not improved by Sludge's obviously relaxed demeanour, as he was actually laughing, having placed his arm around Pamela's shoulders. Joan Sanderson and Beryl Crockford who were standing nearby were also laughing and appeared to be sharing the joke.

Looking around him, Coyne recognised all of the walkers as Society members with the exception of two men, both standing at the back of the group, but at opposite extremes. One was youngish and fresh faced, wearing a green Barbour jacket and the other, an older man he put down to be a friend of Sludge, due solely to the fact that he was wearing a large black hat with a silver band.

'Your attention, please.' he shouted, and clapped his hands with such vigour that he lost his balance and had to step down off the wall in haste. Remounting the wall too quickly, he swayed unsteadily, and had to step down again.

Clambering onto the wall for a third time, he looked down at the woman who had scurried forward to help him, and was now clutching his right leg just above the knee. 'I'm fine.' he assured her in a hoarse whisper recognising her as Betty Turnbull who, at forty-five years of age, was one of the younger members of the Society. 'You can let go now Betty.' Lifting his voice, he announced, 'ladies and gentlemen, welcome to the inaugural walk of the Albert Bleaney Society. This morning,' he wobbled slightly, and Betty, who was frightened he was going to fall again, gripped his leg even tighter. Trying to free himself from her grip caused him to sway dangerously. 'Let go,' he hissed, 'for God's sake woman, let go of my leg.' Even through her thick mittens Betty could feel Ronan's thigh muscles twitching as he fought for balance. Faced with this new and intimate sensation, which she felt bordered on the indecent, Betty did as requested and stepped back, just as Ronan made a determined effort to wrench himself free.

Winded and lying on his back, Ronan looked up at the faces peering over the wall at him. Betty, who couldn't quite rid herself of the sensation of a man's leg moving under her fingers, spoke first. 'Was this his first school then,' she pointed over the recumbent Ronan to the building beyond, 'is this where he went as a child?'

'It is, ' gasped Ronan as he struggled to his feet, 'it certainly is.' Bending over to brush some dirt from his trousers, and to catch his breath, he was horrified to notice that his right trouser leg was torn from the knee downwards, and was now gaping open to show his thin, white, hairless leg.

Acting swiftly, he wrapped his trouser tightly around his leg and pulled up his sock over the trouser to secure it. There was still a noticeable gap, but at least it wouldn't flap about, he convinced himself. He decided to repeat the exercise on the other trouser leg in the belief that it would then look intentional, regretting as he did so his decision to wear the socks with the Mickey Mouse figure on them. Bought because they were very cheap, and, although undignified, he had reasoned no one would ever see them.

On straightening up, he looked around him and discovered his vision was slightly out of focus. The sticking plaster holding his spectacles together had worked loose, the sides were separating and beginning to slide down either side of his nose. Jamming the sides together, he squeezed the plaster around the bridge of his spectacles and after replacing them, declared, 'Nothing much to look at here. There is a map with your itinerary. Our walk is circular; we start here and finish here. Our first stop is the bookshop, then the cemetery, then the house where he listened to records, and so on.' he said. 'But before we set off I want a quick word with my colleague.'

Although Sludge tried to reassure Pamela that her slip was of little consequence as the find had already been destroyed, he was concerned to learn that Ronan knew that 'something' had been found at the late poet's house. He considered Ronan to be an avid self-publicist and unprincipled careerist who would publish any material linked, however marginally, to Albert Bleaney, without regard to its potential effect on the status of the poet.

If Ronan had knowledge of the find of the pubic hair, he would give the information to the press, no doubt with some tenuous links to one or two poems. Such links are easily made, thought Sludge, there is a whole industry devoted to just that. He imagined that the broadsheets would pontificate along the lines that the find indicated, 'the essentially Rabelaisian nature of the poet', whereas the tabloids would simply scream 'pervert'. Sludge feared, such is the nature of newspaper readership and distribution, that would mean a minority would consider the facts and form their own view on the 'Rabelaisian analysis' while a substantial majority would unhesitatingly accept that Albert Bleaney was a pervert.

To stop that from happening he must convince Ronan that the find was both something and nothing. Sludge knew that would not be easy. Ronan's overweening self-importance would insist on knowing the detail, and his predilection for histrionic behaviour, which included quite dramatic tantrums, would probably be unavoidable if he was denied that detail. Yesterday's encounter with Mr Barbour and the forthcoming meeting with Cuthbert, Dibble and Grubb were preoccupying Sludge. The very last thing he felt he needed was a confrontation with Ronan, who, at that moment, was heading towards him with an angry and purposeful air. An air that was somewhat offset by flashing glimpses of bare leg, and further undermined by his spectacles drooping either side of his nose.

Sludge turned as a hand touched his shoulder to see Doc Holliday, who smiled and touched his hat, 'Good morning, Dr Ludgeworth.' he said.

'Good morning, Dr Holliday,' he replied with mock formality, 'I thought you had decided to call me Billy.'

'Ah, you English are so informal. Take this gentleman for instance;' he nodded towards the approaching Ronan Coyne, 'the leader of this walk I believe, a position of some responsibility is it not, and yet look at his dress. His outlandish socks, so prominently displayed, his unseemly trousers, the spots of red paper on his face, his unique spectacles and, yes, the final touch, the unruly hair decorated with what appears to be several blades of grass.' He looked at Ronan who had stopped a short distance away and was staring at Sludge. 'We must talk Billy', he went on, 'I have something to tell you, and I need some information from you. Can we miss the first part of the walk? I noticed a small cafe just around the corner, I'd like to buy you a coffee.'

His determination to confront Sludge challenged by the appearance of the forbidding stranger in the black hat, Ronan Coyne halted his charge some yards away from the pair and glared at Sludge while wondering what to do next.

Sludge turned aside from holding Ronan's manic stare, 'You are a man of surprises, Doc, I never expected irony.' he smiled. 'Coffee is an excellent idea; we can pick up the walk at the cemetery in about forty-five minutes.'

With mounting fury, Ronan Coyne watched the pair walk away. Unable to contain his frustration, he jumped both feet off the ground and stamped them down so fiercely his spectacles fell off. 'I know your secret, Ludgeworth,' he shouted in a shrill voice, 'I know everything.'

If Sludge had turned around, he would have noticed Ronan Coyne's antics had attracted the obvious interest of a fresh-faced young man wearing a green Barbour jacket. A couple of minutes later Ronan Coyne and Mr Barbour could have been seen deep in conversation while hurrying together to join the waiting walkers.

The Empire Tea Rooms

Standing on the corner of Main Street and Florence Avenue, the Empire Tea Rooms was managed by a young couple obsessed with the styles and fashions of the years preceding the 1939/1945 World War. Known as The Empire Tea Rooms since the days when the red of the British Empire dominated the world map, other than the changes wrought by the passing of time, little had changed since the place became a Tea Rooms in the early 1930s. The only alterations they had made since they acquired the business a couple of years ago - apart from restoring the faded décor to its former glory - was to widen the range of coffees and teas available, and to introduce a menu featuring vegetarian and vegan alternatives.

At first, the burghers of Ottingham came to the café out of curiosity because the proprietors, Colin and Terry, were the first openly gay couple to set up in the village. With their curiosity satisfied the initial visitors returned and became regular customers because of the excellent food and the warm and welcoming ambience created by the hosts. The Empire Tea Rooms had also become popular with students who lived in the Eleanor Stark Halls of Residence a short distance away.

'Nice place, Billy,' Doc Holliday looked around the room, 'nothing like this in Boulder, Colorado.' he grinned. Sludge nodded and sipped his coffee carefully, his tongue was still tender and the coffee was very hot.

'Recognise the music?' Sludge asked. Playing softly in the background, a light voice, soft and smooth, was singing to the accompaniment of what was once called a dance band. 'Not your era, I suppose?' The music wasn't Sludge's era either, but his grandparents had been keen dancers and he had grown up to a background of crooners and dance bands.

Turning his head to the side apparently to concentrate on the music Sludge's companion tapped out the rhythm on the table top. 'No, not my era,' he said, 'the singer is Al Bowlly,' he paused, 'and the song is, *'Stay On The Right*

Side Of The Road'. OK?', he smiled, and held out his hand.

'I'm impressed,' said Sludge, shaking the outstretched hand, 'first irony, and now this. Is there no end to your talents?' he laughed. Both men relaxed and sat in silence enjoying the music, and, Sludge was aware, each other's company.

A couple of minutes passed before the silence between them was broken. 'Your suspension is lifted from nine o'clock Monday morning, Billy'. Doc Holliday said quietly, while slowly stirring his coffee. 'Badowski will be in touch before then, either by telephone or messenger.' He lifted his head to look at Sludge, who was staring at him in disbelief. 'Naturally you want to know the how-and-why, but Badowski will explain everything.'

The cold-eyed man drew in a long breath and exhaled slowly. This was good news. But he needed information now. Badowski was a nice guy, but someone had pulled his strings and he had danced. The cold-eyed man knew that he had to talk to the string puller.

Sludge sighed and glanced across the room. He counted the tables, twelve in all, four occupied and eight empty. He thought that he recognised a boy and girl sitting in the corner near the window as first year university students; they weren't in his classes, but he had seen them about campus. Sometimes the vulnerability of those young people affected him so much he could hardly bear it. Still looking across the room he said, 'Why me, Doc?'

'It's not for you Billy. I told you when we first met, it's for Fabio Brindisi.'

'Doc, if you can get my legitimate and justified suspension lifted, then I am sure that you could find a very easy way to get Fabio Brindisi through graduation, so, why me?' Sludge placed his hand on his chest, 'Why are you helping *me*?' he said.

Tilting his cup, Doc Holliday appeared to inspect the contents carefully while saying, 'Am I helping you?'

'Doc,' said Sludge, placing both hands flat on the table, ' in the past few days my life has been disrupted. Yes, I know partly my own fault,' he said with a touch of impatience, directed at himself rather than his companion, 'but disrupted nevertheless. If the suspension and possible prosecution and loss of my job were not enough, I have Fabio and you on my back, to say nothing of MI5 or whoever they are, following me about.' There was also of course, his decision to kill Poisonous Pete he thought, looking across at his companion who had raised his eyes and was smiling.

'MI5?' he said. 'The young man in the Barbour jacket, no doubt. Why are they following you?'

Sludge ignored the enquiry, 'Why are *you* helping *me*?' he persisted.

Still smiling, Doc Holliday removed his wallet from an inside pocket and laid it unopened on the table. 'I will keep a long story very short.' he said. 'In my line of work you get asked to do some unusual things. A little under two years ago, Paulo Brindisi asked me to check out a particular university on the north east coast of England because he was planning to send his son there. I wasn't too impressed with what I found until I came across your name.' He opened his wallet and removed a newspaper clipping that he carefully unfolded. 'I was pretty busy at the time and I took a short cut, I reckoned that if it was good enough for you, then it was certainly good enough for the Brindisi boy.'

'I don't understand,' said Sludge, 'what do you know of me?'

By way of reply Doc Holliday passed the clipping across the table. Sludge was astounded to find he was looking at the photograph of the students facing the National Guard, taken from the Dallas Morning News, June 7th 1985. Leaning forward Doc Holliday indicated the central figure, 'This of course is you, and this,' he pointed to a bearded figure with shoulder length hair at the back of the photograph, 'is me.' Sitting back in his seat he smiled again, 'I guess I've changed more than you.'

Sludge looked up from the photograph, 'No doubt about that,' he said, 'no doubt at all.' He peered again at the photograph, 'I'm sorry, I don't remember you.'

'We spoke no more than a couple of times.' said Doc Holliday ' I wasn't in your classes,' he added by way of explanation, 'my girl friend, Birdy Kaplanski, was one of your students.'

Sludge was staring at the photograph with unseeing eyes. He remembered Birdy Kaplanski, she was nicknamed Birdy because she was small, bright eyed and lively. She was a good student, she was also one of the protesters injured by the National Guard.

'I remember Birdy,' said Sludge, 'she was hurt during the demonstration. I remember visiting her in the hospital just before I was declared *persona non grata* and thrown out of the country. What happened?'

'What happened?' Doc Holliday took out a large white handkerchief and wiped his lips and moustache. 'Birdy and a number of others were expelled for their part in the protest. The rest of us, or as many as they could find, were suspended and fined. After you had gone, we had no one to speak for us and the University more or less did as they wanted to, or were ordered to by the Government. Yes, I'm still a conspiracy theorist.' he grinned at Sludge. 'Birdy was in hospital for a couple of weeks or so, and then went home to Chicago; we lost touch after a while.'

'Those were very difficult times,' Sludge reflected, 'for a lot of people.' He thought of his own return to England, and the subsequent years that he could not claim had been either fruitful or even enjoyable. He shivered slightly, 'And you,' he said, 'how did you get into this line of work, whatever it is that you do.'

'There's no doubt that the events of June '85 sent me down a different road from that I had planned. I travelled extensively and eventually became what I am.'

'And that is?' Sludge enquired.

'I haven't got a regular job description,' Doc Holliday responded with a wry smile, 'I am involved with a worldwide organisation that doesn't seek or need publicity. I suppose you could say that I am a sort of international co-ordinator, which brings me to the point of wanting some information from you. I have been asked to check something on behalf of an associate in Madrid.' He looked around the room before asking in a low voice, 'Tell me what you know about Dr Peter Pelham.'

The cold-eyed man froze on hearing Pelham's name. He was suddenly aware of danger. What possible connection could there be between Pelham and the man from Colorado? What was the mysterious worldwide organisation? He was painfully aware that Doc Holliday operated in a different sphere of what-was-possible. Great care was needed.

'I know that he is a colleague.' said Sludge quietly.

'This song is very special to me.' said Doc Holliday, as Al Bowlly began to sing, *Buddy, Can You Spare a Dime?*. 'My grandparents were dust bowl farmers in the thirties, I've always imagined that this song was about them.' Both men sat silently, listening to the words of the song. When it had finished Doc Holliday, who had been staring at the table looked up at Sludge, 'Your reticence about Dr Pelham is to your credit,' he said, 'but tell me, is it born out of loyalty, or circumspection?'

'Loyalty - to Pelham? No, not that.' said Sludge with an emphasis that revealed more than his words.

'Well then,' said Doc Holliday, 'let me test your caution. I will keep this brief. A colleague in Madrid has a daughter studying at your university. She has told her father that Pelham has propositioned her. Apparently, if she will consent to what my countrymen call a quickie, she will pass; if she doesn't consent, she will fail. Sex for marks, it's as simple as that.' He glanced at his wristwatch, 'Do we have time for another coffee?'

Sludge shook his head, 'We need to be leaving in a minute or two. What do you want from me?'

'I want you to give me a straightforward answer to this question.' Doc Holliday said briskly, 'How likely is it that Pelham would have made such a demand? In addition to that I want your view on something.' He paused while the waiter cleared the coffee cups from the table, shook his head at the offer of another drink. 'A Japanese girl, Julie Wang, died two years ago.' he said flatly, 'Was Pelham involved? My information contradicts the official version, but I want your opinion.'

The cold-eyed man took his time lighting his cigarette. The cards had been played and were on the table. But it might be a crooked deal. He squinted through the smoke at the man from Colorado whose face told him nothing. He made a decision. He would play the cards he held.

'Could Pelham have made such a demand?' said Sludge, 'Yes, he could. Was he involved in the death of Julie Wang? In my opinion, almost certainly.'

A commotion in the street outside attracted the attention of both men who turned to see a very red faced Ronan Coyne waving wildly to a small group of Albert Bleaney devotees. Standing patiently to one side of the manic Ronan, a phlegmatic Mr Barbour looked about him with a casual air, noticed the observers in the Empire Tea Rooms, but gave no indication that he had done so.

'Thanks for that Billy.' Doc Holliday stood up, 'I won't mention him again.' he said, handing Sludge his hat. 'Shall we join the walk, it looks as though it's beginning to get exciting.' He peered through the window at Ronan,

'I don't suppose you know why he has a yellow and green ribbon tied to his arm,' he said 'is it a badge of office?'

'That man is a fool,' said Sludge calmly and without rancour, 'a complete and utter fool.' Opening the door, he glanced down the street. 'They have left the bookshop and appear to be heading for the cemetery. Shall we walk along at the back?' he said as he watched Ronan Coyne, leaping with all the grace of a floundering fish, narrowly avoid being run down by an irate cyclist.

NINE

The Walk continues

'Excuse me,' Ronan turned from staring at the back of the retreating Sludge and his mysterious, moustachioed friend in the hat, to see that he was being addressed by a smart young man wearing a green Barbour jacket, 'your spectacles appear to be damaged,' he said, 'perhaps I can help.' Ronan put his hand to his face and seemed bewildered by the absence of his spectacles. 'On the grass.' said the young man helpfully. Bending down he retrieved the separate pieces and handed them to Ronan whose anger had given way to confusion.

'I suggest that you strap this stick along the top of your spectacles, and bind it into place with the sticking plaster'. Mr Barbour held out a small twig (from which, drawing on his training in the deployment of natural resources, he had stripped leaves and bark) to a doubtful looking Ronan Coyne. 'Here,' he said, 'give them to me'. Taking the two pieces of the spectacles, Mr Barbour efficiently bound them to the twig making use of a long thin strip of bark as well as the sticking plaster. 'Not very pretty, I'm afraid,' he said, 'but it will do until you can get them fixed.' He smiled encouragingly as Ronan tested the repair. 'I'm Jeremy Barbour,' he said holding out his hand, 'I'm looking forward to this walk. Do you mind if I come along with you?'

'I'm Dr Coyne', he said, shaking the outstretched hand, 'let's join the others.' he added, as he squinted uncertainly at the helpful young man.

Ahead of them, the group, headed by Joan and Beryl, were heading down a narrow side street in the general direction of the centre of Ottingham. Turning to check on the whereabouts of Ronan, Joan smiled at the incongruity of what she saw. She noted how the calm athletic grace of the tall young man in the Barbour emphasised the manic hyperactivity of the ill-dressed Ronan Coyne.

Striding easily alongside his scurrying companion, Mr Barbour reflected on Ronan's outburst. He glanced at the small dishevelled figure and wondered how best to learn what he knew; according to the eruption directed at Ludgeworth, Ronan Coyne' 'knew everything'. Barbour was keenly aware that the sooner he resolved the puzzle, then the sooner he could get out of this place. In addition to that, he would have succeeded where others had failed, and that would be worth a few points in the career stakes. 'I must be careful,' he thought, 'the highly strung clown will break if I push too hard, he's obviously near the edge. But I must find out what he knows.'

'Everyone stop!' Ronan shouted, turning and holding up his hand. He had set a fast pace and the group had become strung out behind him. The suddenness of his action caused a minor pile up as the chattering walkers at the back, who hadn't heard the instruction, continued walking and bumped into each other. The resultant ripple effect reached Meredith Winstanley, a balding man with a black goatee beard standing at the front of the pack, propelling him forward with some force and causing him to lose his balance and pitch headlong into Ronan Coyne. As his head struck Ronan smartly in the lower abdomen, thereby cushioning his fall, he was saved from serious injury.

'Terribly sorry, Ronan old boy,' he gasped, looking with concern at the white face of Ronan who was sitting on the ground immediately in front of him with both hands clutched between his legs, 'you saved me from a nasty fall there.'

'Ahhh! Ahhh!' groaned Ronan, 'Please,' he gasped, 'everyone into the car park here.' Still sitting on the ground he moved one hand from his groin and waved it in a general direction to his right. 'I'll tell you where we are going. Ah yes, thank you.' he acknowledged the assistance of Mr Barbour who helped him to stand up.

The car park was small and the walkers standing shoulder to shoulder made it impossible for Ronan to get the distance he needed to address them. Seeing his difficulty, Mr Barbour suggested that, as the road was narrow, he could take up a position on the side directly opposite. Ronan was beginning to appreciate the help of the young man and crossed the road. Once there he realised that he still couldn't see everyone as he was finding it difficult to stand up straight, so he climbed the three steps up to the front door of a private house. 'Yes, that's much better.' he nodded at Mr Barbour, as the door behind him was opened by a large man wearing a black tracksuit and red training shoes.

'What do you want?' A deep voice growled in Ronan's ear.

'Ah, well', began Ronan, 'we're,' he pointed across the road, 'we're going...'

'Clear off.' The owner of the deep voice interrupted, 'Get off my property or I'll throw you off.' He glared at Ronan, taking in the decorated spectacles and the state of his trousers, 'Not Rag Week again!' he said, 'You bloody students are all the same!'

'We're not…'

'Clear off!' The man shouted, as he stepped forward menacingly.

'Follow me.' Ronan called across the road as he ran awkwardly, but speedily down the steps and out of the front gate, catching the cuff of his left sleeve on the gate latch as he did so, ripping it almost to the elbow. 'Damn and blast,' he said, looking at the damage, 'damn and blast.'

'Where are we going Ronan?' enquired Meredith Winstanley, nervously tugging at his beard.

'To Mr Bleaney's bookshop,' said Ronan, 'follow me, it's just a few minutes away on Main Street. Follow me.' He waved the group forward revealing that his arm, although surprisingly sinewy, was as white and hairless as his leg, of which more and more could be glimpsed as the trick with his sock began to lose its effectiveness.

Mr Barbour decided that further involvement in Ronan's growing catalogue of disasters would distract him from his main purpose. He watched in silent fascination as Ronan unwound his long woollen scarf from around his neck and then removed his necktie, a sickly affair in yellow and green, which he placed in his pocket while he replaced his scarf. Taking the tie out of his pocket, he held it out to Mr Barbour, 'Do me the honours,' he said, holding out his left arm from which the remnants of his sleeve dangled, 'wrap it round, stop the sleeve flapping about.' he explained.

'Certainly.' responded the young man, running the necktie several times around Ronan's sleeve before tying it in an unnecessarily flamboyant bow. They walked together in silence for a few moments before the young man spoke again, 'I found your comment to Ludgeworth intriguing.' he said, 'What is the secret, can you tell me?'

'Do you know Ludgeworth?' said Ronan, a sharp edge to his voice that Mr Barbour noticed.

'Know him? Not really,' he replied, 'we've met a couple of times briefly. I am studying the life and times of Albert Bleaney; I went to him for some advice, and I have to say he wasn't very helpful at all.'

'You should have come to me.' said Ronan dismissively, 'I know everything there is to know about Albert Bleaney.'

Mr Barbour smiled as he glanced across at Ronan and reminded himself to treat the strange little man with care. 'I realise that,' he said smoothly, 'but he lives around here and you don't. I was in this area on business and so took a chance. I'm very lucky that I could stay for the walk,' he smiled again and placed his hand on Ronan's shoulder, 'and to have the opportunity to meet you and to ask for your help.'

Ronan was flattered by the attention of the young man. Although he was a man of indiscriminate taste in his dress, he recognised taste and quality in others, and there was a casual elegance and confidence about the young man that proclaimed 'county set' to Ronan, who was undeniably a snob. 'What is it you want to know?' he said.

'Well,' said Mr Barbour, 'as a student of Bleaney's work I have a long list, but could you satisfy my curiosity first. The secret,' he went on, 'what is Ludgeworth's secret?' He glanced across the road in an attempt to indicate that the question was not of primary importance and was surprised to see a shop window with a prominent Gieves and Hawkes advertisement. 'A sign of former better times,' he thought to himself, 'I'll look in later.'

'The secret?' Oh, yes, I know the secret.' Ronan said. 'Wait a minute, we're at the shop.' He turned into a dusty arcade of eight shops, four on each side, only two of which appeared to be open for business. Taking up a position at the head of the arcade, he directed people towards the shop. Raising his voice, he called, 'Everyone gather in front of the shop at the bottom on the right.' He looked up the street to see that Beryl and Joan, who were deep in conversation, had fallen some way behind. 'Hurry up, you two,' he shouted, 'hurry up.'

Joan looked at the distant waving figure of Ronan with disapproval. 'Look at the state of him.' she said, 'Who does he think he is?'

'I don't know why we are going down that place,' said Beryl, 'to the best of my knowledge Albert never went there. He complained when the old chapel was demolished so that the arcade could be built. He always bought his books at the shop in the city centre, where June used to work. If he came here at all it was to buy home made curd cheesecakes from Mackman's shop at the top of the street.'

'Ronan wouldn't know that.' said Joan disparagingly. 'He might know the poems after a fashion, but he didn't know Albert, or anything about him. '

Even though they were now within twenty yards of the arcade, Ronan continued to gesticulate excitedly. 'Whatever would Albert have made of him?' said Beryl with evident distaste.

'He would have seen through him and wouldn't have had anything to do with him.' said Joan with conviction, before laughing, 'If he saw the way he is today he would have crossed to the other side of the road as quickly as possible.'

'Right, we're all here, at last.' said Ronan as he moved down the arcade to stand in front of a large plate glass window that was cracked across one corner. A notice was pasted on the window announcing that the proprietors had moved out some three years earlier. Ronan pointed at the dirty and almost derelict shop, which was empty, save for a mound of unopened junk mail and catalogues. 'It was here,' he said, rubbing the grimy window with his hand the better to peer into the shop, 'that Albert Bleaney sometimes bought books.'

The motley group of people - Sludge had once suggested that a suitable collective noun for members of a dead poet's society was 'a shroud' - that was standing in a semi circle three or four deep looked at the decrepit shop with an awkward reverence. To everyone's relief, after a lengthy and embarrassing silence, Betty Turnbull stepped forward with a camera in her hand and asked Ronan to stand near the shop door so that she could take his photograph. Ronan was glad to oblige and struck a pose, gripping the door handle with his left hand, right hand on his hip, right foot turned outwards. Allowing a discreet smile to play around his lips, he held the position while several of the walkers followed Betty's example.

The young man in the green Barbour jacket surveyed the scene with a growing sense of disbelief. People were now jostling each other to take photographs of a lunatic posing in front of a dirty and empty shop where a poet (now dead) may or may not have bought the occasional book. 'I've got to force things,' he thought as Ronan Coyne showed no signs of moving on, 'I'm getting nowhere.'

'Time is our enemy, Dr Coyne.' he announced as he stepped forward to take Ronan's arm. Leading him forcefully from the door, he said, 'We are waiting for your instructions, where are we heading for now?' He led Ronan to the top of the arcade before releasing his grip.

'Don't manhandle me.' protested Ronan in a squeaky whisper.

'Tell people where they are going.' said the young man coldly.

Ronan looked at the young man, and then at the crowd gathered behind him. 'We're going to the cemetery.' he called out in a sulky voice. He was unhappy that Mr Barbour had intervened while people were still taking photographs. He wasn't even a member of the Society, he thought bitterly. 'This way,' he pointed down the street, 'turn left at the bottom.'

To Ronan's great surprise and alarm, Mr Barbour stepped forward, grasped his arm once more, and said in a loud voice, 'Follow us'. He began to march down the street with the somewhat reluctant Ronan by his side. 'Lead on MacDuff,' he whispered in Ronan's ear without a trace of humour, 'and set a good pace.' Small groups of two and three people began to follow Ronan and Mr Barbour, but a growing crowd was gathering round Beryl and Joan, who were still at the top of the arcade and were pointing in the opposite direction to that indicated by Ronan.

'Mackman's', said Joan, 'up on the right, just past the chemist, that's where Albert Bleaney used to buy his curd cheesecakes'. She gazed pensively towards the shop, 'He loved them.' she added softly, almost to herself.

'Did he ever write about curd cheesecakes?' asked Elsie Battle, a small, sharp-nosed woman with bulbous eyes. 'Did he, Brian?' She turned to a tall, thin man wearing a yellow cagoule. Brian Crispey knew all of Bleaney's poems very well; in fact he knew a large number by heart, and was looking forward to reciting *Killing Time*, the poet's observations on the relationship between work and death, in the cemetery.

'No,' he replied, 'he never did.' Brian regretted wearing his yellow cagoule, but his mother, a fierce woman of eighty-five years of age, had insisted it was going to rain. He had looked doubtfully at the blue sky, but had accepted his mother's word, as he knew from long experience not to contradict her views on either the weather or eating habits. 'I haven't had a curd cheesecake for years.' he said wistfully.

'Really?' said Beryl, 'that is a shame. I've got an idea,' she said enthusiastically, 'why don't we go to Mackman's now and buy one? If nothing else, it will be more interesting than gazing at a dusty old shop.'

'Yes, let's do that,' Joan agreed, 'we've got plenty of time.'

'This is an excellent idea.' enthused Elsie Battle, clapping her bony hands with delight and hopping from one foot to the other. 'We can all buy curd cheesecakes and take them to the cemetery and eat them near Albert Bleaney's grave.' She clasped her hands to her chest and smiled brightly, glad that the strange gloom of the arcade had been dispersed.

The small band, keen to walk in the steps of the late poet, set off eagerly for the cake shop. Unaware that Ronan Coyne had noticed the splinter group, and was shouting and gesticulating at them, they continued on their quest chattering happily together.

Ronan Coyne was angry that Mr Barbour was acting in such a peremptory manner and intended to put him in his place at the first opportunity. But for the moment, he had noticed that a number of the walkers, apparently led by Joan and Beryl, were heading in completely the wrong direction. Wrenching his arm free of Mr Barbour's grasp, he stepped into the middle of the street and shouted, 'Come back. Come back.' he waved his arms and shouted again, 'You're going the wrong way. Oh!' he exclaimed, jumping awkwardly back onto the pavement as a cyclist swerved round him shouting loudly into Ronan's face as he did so.

'Bloody student!' the cyclist cried, shaking his fist as peddled furiously down the street.

Shaken by the action of the cyclist Ronan leaned against the window of a hairdresser's shop and tried to recover his equilibrium. 'Shall I go and get them?' volunteered Meredith Winstanley, who, having butted Ronan in the stomach earlier, was anxious to make amends.

'Oh, yes, yes please,' gasped Ronan, 'meet us at the cemetery,' he pointed up the street, 'up here, go left and it's on the left.'

'Oi, you,' Ronan turned to find he was being addressed by a young girl wearing what appeared to be a lilac boiler suit open almost to the waist to reveal an improbable amount of pink flesh, her large red lips surprisingly outlined in a deeper shade of red, 'get off the window,' she demanded, 'you've been told before.' She peered suspiciously at Ronan, lifting her eyebrows at his peculiar state of dress, 'You're a bit old for a student aren't you,' she laughed scornfully, 'anyway, whoever you are, get off the window or I'll call the police.'

Not trusting himself to speak and conscious of his rapidly beating heart, Ronan straightened up from the window and saw that he was being observed from the other side of the street by Sludge and his friend in the hat. His felt his bile rising as he saw the faintly mocking smile on Sludge's face.

He was about to charge across the road to confront him, when once more he felt his arm gripped very firmly. 'Be careful of the traffic.' said Mr Barbour as he directed Ronan away from the shop. The young man had also noticed Sludge and his companion. 'Let's get a move on Dr Coyne,' he said, 'now, what was that secret you were going to tell me?'

'You're hurting my arm.' complained Ronan. Due to the firmness with which the young man was gripping his arm, Ronan had to twist his head around to look behind him. He noticed that all the walkers who had followed him from the arcade had joined the bearded man in his search for the rest of the group, and were now heading back in the direction they had come from. 'What on earth is going on?' he groaned.

'Don't worry,' said Mr Barbour, 'we will all meet up at the cemetery. While we are waiting you can tell me what you know.' he said, not smiling, neither did he relinquish his grip on Ronan's arm.

Meredith Winstanley was out of breath when he arrived at Mackman's cake shop in time to see a group, who all appeared to be clutching paper bags, gathered around Joan Sanderson and Beryl Crockford.

'What's all this?' he gasped, 'Ronan wants us,' he pointed, 'down there.'

'This is where Mr Bleaney bought his curd cheesecakes,' said Elsie Battle, 'we've all bought some, and we are going to eat them at the cemetery.' she added with a note of defiance aimed at the distant Ronan Coyne.

Meredith had travelled up from Nottingham that morning and before setting out had prepared his favourite sandwiches, thick slices of wholemeal bread, cheddar cheese and lashings of pickle, these, together with a slice of Bakewell tart, he had placed carefully in a Tupperware container. He sighed heavily as he thought of his meticulously prepared lunch that, due to a momentary lapse in concentration caused by the arrival of the post, was still on the kitchen table in Nottingham. He looked hungrily at Mackman's window, which contained not only fancy cakes, but also a range of cheeses, and a hand written notice announcing, 'Sandwiches Made To Order'.

Ten minutes later, Meredith and the others who had followed him on his errand, were holding paper bags and listening to Beryl; who, having waited for them to make their purchases, was talking to the whole group and suggesting an alternative route to the Cemetery.

'This lane,' Beryl and Joan had moved the group to the rear of Mackman's where a small lane twisted around a corner, 'leads to a path alongside some allotments. The path then runs past the Cemetery before coming out on De La Pole Road in West Kingston.'

'Isn't that near where Albert Bleaney lived?' interrupted Brian Crispey.

'Ah, good to see you know your geography as well as your poetry.' Beryl smiled. 'Yes, it is near West Bank. As it was Joan's idea to walk along this path perhaps she would like to add something.'

By way of reply, Joan walked slowly down the lane, leading the group to an old wooden picket fence and large five-barred gate with a notice proclaiming that the allotments within were the property of Ottingham RDC and forbidding entry to unauthorised users.

'Fortunately we're not going in there,' she laughed, and pointed to a wide path leading off to the right, 'we're going this way, along Top Path. In mediaeval times this was the route the farmers took to the market in Kingston. Albert told me that,' she said, 'many years ago. It's called Top Path,' she added, catching an enquiring glance from Elsie Battle who was busily writing in a small note book, 'because it's higher than Bottom Path, which is on the other side of the village. Or so Albert said.' she went on, looking at the earnest faces around her she wondered, not for the first time, why it seemed to be a requirement that the love of poetry should be such a serious business.

Lost in thought the group looked at the ancient path, which gradually dropped away from them. Bordered on either side by an old hawthorn hedge, just coming into blossom, that formed a canopy over the path in midsummer as each side reached out to greet the other. To the left the allotments offered a vista of ramshackle sheds and neatly tended vegetable plots with, here and there, a sudden splash of colour from a rogue flowerbed. To the right the higgledy-piggledy backs of the shops and houses of Main Street. In front of them a short distance away the cemetery could be glimpsed through the protecting barrier of oak, elm and ash, and then the beginnings of Kingston, undistinguishable now from the village; and beyond the town, unseen, the plain of Aulderness and then the cold unwelcoming North Sea.

'Did Mr Bleaney come down here then?'

Joan looked at the speaker, the Reverend Peter Meadows, a retired vicar from Doncaster. 'Yes, it was one of his favourite walks,' she said, 'a long time ago'.

The implications of her reply were not lost on her audience several of whom determined to reread the poems as soon as possible to try to identify this location and to search for concealed meaning. As they already knew, that was a vain hope, as Albert Bleaney had never published any poems about his personal relationships.

'He used to cycle along here too.' said Beryl. 'He would come this way to Mackman's on his trusty old bike.' she laughed, 'He left that bike to Billy - Dr Ludgeworth, that is. Perhaps we should have asked him to bring it today. We could have taken turns.' she said, still laughing.

'Is it far to the cemetery?' said Betty Turnbull. 'Only Dr Coyne seemed to be getting agitated, and I don't think we should be late.'

'We will be there before him.' said Joan confidently. 'The cemetery curves around towards us,' she pointed down the track, 'we will enter almost exactly where Albert's grave stands. The others, if there are any others,' she said looking around, 'will go in at the far end and have to walk a long way to get to Albert's grave. Don't worry we will be there first.'

'Oh dear, I think that will upset him even more.' said Betty Turnbull, a worried frown crossing her face.

At Maudy Cemetery

Due to a singular lack of imagination by the municipal planners, Maudy Cemetery was situated off a thoroughfare called Cemetery Road. According to local historians, there had been a burial place on the site dating back to Anglo Saxon times. The earliest readable headstone referred to Betsey, the wife of Michael Andrew, who died May 12th 1795, aged thirty, 'She was a virtuous wife, a dutiful daughter, an indulgent mother and a good friend.' There was the usual horrifying crop of child deaths from the good old days of the 19th century. The Coombs family suffered particularly badly: Elizabeth Coombs, who departed this life June 29th 1849 (2 months); Elizabeth Goldworthy Coombs, June 10th 1853 (2 years 7 months); John William Coombs, February 19th 1857 (3 months); Elizabeth Selina Coombs, April 30th 1857 (3 years); Thomas Coombs, May 24th 1857 (4 years 2 months); 'Look up, look up and weep no more / Thy darling is not dead'. Dominating a far corner, a First Great War memorial was dedicated to the East Riding

Pals, mainly young farm labourers from the area who had apparently found peace in the mud of Ypres, Passenchendaele and the Somme.

A central driveway led down to a small Victorian chapel, behind that was a later crematorium. Winding paths led off the drive between trees of oak and ash, yew and willow, opening to clearings with twenty or thirty headstones in each, some for families, some for a particular period. Beyond the paths and the clearings was an open space of more uniform pattern, where the dead were laid out in neat rows as though waiting for yet another last trump.

The Bleaney family had a small plot, acquired in the last century, in a clearing almost completely enclosed by hawthorn and crab apple. It was here that Albert Bleaney closed the third generation of Bleaneys, when he joined his parents and grandparents to lie alongside his brother. Due to special provision in his will, as there were no Bleaneys to follow him, Molly Ripley had taken the final place some yards away. Still awaiting a headstone, Molly's place was marked by a rectangle of white stones and a marble vase.

Standing in respectful silence beneath boughs heavy with blossom, the members of the Albert Bleaney Society contemplated the simple white stone that read, 'Albert Bleaney (1935-1997) Poet', and listened as Brian Crispey came to the end of the much-anthologised Bleaney poem, *Killing Time*. Each with their own thoughts, clutching Mackman's bags and feeling the warmth of freshly baked curd cheesecakes on their fingers, they also pondered the propriety of eating cakes in such a place.

'He was simply / Killing time,' Brian said, pausing to look around him before delivering the final chilling lines, 'Until the arrival/Of the time to die.'

A few minutes earlier, an altercation had taken place on the other side of the cemetery. Ronan Coyne had become increasingly desperate under Mr Barbour's insistent and progressively aggressive questioning. He couldn't answer the questions because he didn't know Sludge's secret, but he couldn't bring himself to admit that, and so employed evasive tactics that had served only to increase Barbour's anger, at which the younger man tightened his already clamp like grip on Ronan's arm, causing him to gasp with pain.

With a great effort Ronan wrenched himself free and stepped backwards, away from his tormentor, 'A secret is a secret,' he shouted, 'you will have to wait for the book to come out, just like everyone else.' He rubbed his arm gingerly while trying to hold the other's implacable stare. Ronan Coyne was a fool; he also had a very large ego, an unfortunate combination that led him to an error that was to have disastrous consequences. 'Of course,' he said, 'it is possible that you will not have to wait until then,' he stopped rubbing his arm, and striking a pose, he gripped the lapel of his jacket, 'it depends if I can hold off the literary correspondents for the *Times* and the *Guardian*, among others.'

Warming to his theme he failed to notice the look of horror his comments had brought to Barbour's face. 'Oh, yes,' he said airily, ' they know I can produce the goods and they have got wind of a Bleaney story somehow linked to his OBE, so they have approached me.' He was now holding both lapels and taking small steps backwards and forwards as his fabrication became real to him. 'I am very experienced with the media and can probably persuade them to wait, but this story could be very big indeed.' He puffed out his cheeks and turned to look into the middle distance as he sometimes did in his lectures in the fond hope that his students would see that as intellectual distancing. As he did so he caught sight of the Albert Bleaney Society gathered around Albert Bleaney's grave, some three hundred yards away, 'How did they get here?' he shouted as he began to run towards them, taking the shorter, direct route rather than following the more circuitous route of the paths.

With a growing sense of foreboding, Mr Barbour watched the surprisingly sprightly figure of Ronan Coyne swerving and dodging through the gravestones like a balletic footballer. Yesterday he had failed to get anywhere with Ludgeworth. He knew he had frightened him, but that was all he had achieved. Thus far he had failed to get anywhere at all with this volatile little man. 'Idiot.' he muttered to himself as Ronan temporarily disappeared from view, apparently having tripped over an exposed tree root. He reappeared seconds later, still running, but now limping heavily and, having gone slightly off course, was heading for the densely wooded side of the clearing. 'But a dangerous idiot.' he thought grimly as he began to walk slowly towards the small band in the distance who he could see were standing quite still, heads bowed as if in prayer.

Mr Barbour considered his dilemma; he had been given a mission, he was to find out if a particular object existed and to recover it, while maintaining absolute secrecy. He had been told that in no circumstances could he reveal the object of his quest, in case it didn't exist. He was far from certain that Ludgeworth knew anything and was beginning to conclude that Coyne was blowing hot air, or perhaps referring to some peculiar wrangle inside the Bleaney society, until he had mentioned the newspapers and referred to the poet's OBE. The implication that the 'secret' could have a connection with Bleaney's visit to the palace was deeply worrying as it had direct relevance to his own quest.

A movement to his left attracted his attention and looking across he saw Sludge and Doc Holliday on a parallel path heading to the Bleaney grave. He slowed his pace further so that he would be behind them when the paths converged some way ahead. 'Who *is* that guy with Ludgeworth?' he wondered aloud. His colleagues back at 'head office' had been unable to give any information about him other than his name was undoubtedly an alias and a pointed warning to keep out of his way. Barbour recognised the type, but thought that such a person was very much out of place in this backwater, 'No more so than I am.' he said to himself with a rueful glance around him.

Mr Barbour was a decisive young man. If Ronan Coyne gave the story to the newspapers then his mission would be a complete failure, but only if Coyne's story was the one that Barbour had been told to suppress. He knew that that was a risk he could not take as his reputation and his future were in the balance. He had decided. Ronan Coyne had to be silenced. Strolling down the path with his hands in his pockets and whistling softly to himself, he began to form a strategy.

In the hush that followed Brian Crispey's moving delivery of *Killing Time*, the members of the Albert Bleaney Society became aware of a series of grunts and muttered imprecations as someone - or something - crashed through the undergrowth towards them. As the noise drew closer they glanced nervously at each other while trying to keep an eye on the dense hawthorn hedge that appeared to holding it - whatever it was - at bay.

'There's someone there!' shrieked Elsie Battle, pointing a trembling finger at a section of the hedge that was being shaken violently, and through which the figure of a man could be seen attacking the foliage with a manic energy. Meredith Winstanley was known as a man of action in his part of Nottingham, and he stepped forward to investigate just as Ronan Coyne burst through the hedge with such force that he staggered several paces forward before he tumbled to the ground on his hands and knees, landing on Albert Bleaney's grave, and striking his nose sharply against the headstone.

Ronan levered himself in to a sitting position and noticed that his trouser leg was now torn to the thigh and as a result his bare leg was exposed for all to see. After plucking ineffectually at the cloth in an attempt to rearrange it somehow, he gave up, and dabbing his bleeding nose, peered at the circle of faces that were looking down at him with a mixture of concern and amusement.

'Ronan,' said Beryl sharply, 'please move. You are sitting on Albert's grave.'

Meredith Winstanley stepped forward and placed his hand under Ronan's elbow, 'Come on, old boy,' he said, 'let me help you out of there.'

'Thank you, yes.' Ronan said, struggling to his feet and realising as he did so that his ankle was very painful, probably as a result of him tripping over a few minutes earlier. 'Ouch!' he winced, as he put his weight down,

'Ouch! Ouch!' he said, as he hobbled around Albert's grave, 'Damn and blast! Bugger and botheration! he burst out in exasperation.

'Moderation, Dr Coyne, moderation,' said the Reverend Meadows in authoritative tones, 'remember where you are. This is a place of both great happiness and great sadness. It is not a place for displays of boorishness.'

He looked disdainfully at the dishevelled somewhat pathetic figure now leaning against a tree fiddling with his disgraceful trousers and wondered how such a person could have become an officer of the Bleaney Society. An inveterate joiner of literary societies, John Betjeman, Thomas Hardy and John Clare, among others, received his support, the Reverend Peter Meadows was a veteran of such walks and had quickly realised that this walk was designed to promote Ronan Coyne, rather than honour the memory of a very fine poet.

Ronan Coyne looked around him; two or three people were talking quietly together. Others were inspecting the contents of paper bags. Betty Turnbull was wiping blood off Albert Bleaney's gravestone, while several photographs were taken of her at work, and of the other Bleaney graves. Someone said, 'Isn't Molly Ripley buried near here?'

'Yes, yes,' said Ronan, sensing an opportunity to reassert himself as leader of the group, 'it's just over there. Joan,' he said, failing to notice she had been regarding him with utter distaste, 'go and stand on Molly's grave.'

'I most certainly will not.' said Joan icily, ' I will stand near the grave, but not on it.' So saying she walked across to the rectangle of stones and stood quietly for a few moments while more photographs were taken. 'Ronan,' she said across the small clearing, 'the next stop on your itinerary is 55 Kings Bench Street where, according to your notes, Albert used to visit someone called Jim, to listen to his record collection.' Ronan blinked rapidly and nodded. 'As I understand it,' said Joan, 'the intention is that we are going to stand outside a house that Albert may or may not have visited.' Ronan could feel that his face was still burning at the humiliating comments from Reverend Meadows. His nose was very sore and he was beginning to wonder if he had actually broken his ankle; and, as he was aware that he had made an imaginative leap in connecting Albert Bleaney to 55 Kings Bench Street, he was concerned at the implication behind Joan's question. Not trusting himself to speak, he simply nodded in reply.

'Beryl and I,' Joan continued in response to his nod, 'who knew Albert for a great many years, know nothing of someone called 'Jim', nor of any connection with 55 Kings Bench Street.'

Billy Sludge, who with Doc Holliday had joined the group in time to witness the exchange between Joan and Ronan, broke the ensuing embarrassed silence. Although he had taken no part in the planning of the walk, Sludge, as an original member of the Albert Bleaney Society, felt a degree of responsibility. He sensed that Joan's questioning had an unspoken agenda.

'Do you have an alternative Joan?' he asked quietly.

'Yes, we have.' said Beryl, glancing first at Joan and then across at Ronan who was still leaning against a tree and obviously preoccupied, 'On our way down Top Path Joan happened to point out the Lady le Gros public house down by the Beck and mentioned that her and Albert used to go there. I also went there with him several times. He was a creature of habit.' she smiled. 'It's only about ten minutes from here. As there are tables outside we thought we would go there for a picnic lunch,' she held up a Mackman's bag containing a curd cheesecake, 'and Brian had kindly offered to let us hear some more of Albert's verse.'

'Sounds like a good idea,' said Sludge, 'what do you think Ronan?'

'If anyone is interested in what I think,' said Ronan peevishly, dabbing at his nose as it steadily dripped blood, '55 Kings Bench Street is an official part of the walk and the Lady le Gros isn't. But far be it for me to interfere with what people want to do. If they would rather drink beer than visit an important place in Bleaney's life,' he paused to make an emphatic gesture with his right arm and overbalanced, causing him to cry out in pain as he inadvertently put all his weight on his injured ankle. 'I will be going to 55 Kings Bench Street,' he said faintly as beads of perspiration formed on his forehead, 'if you want to come with me, please raise your hand.' He surveyed the group anxiously; those who were looking at him saw that in mopping his brow with his bloody handkerchief he had left a succession of red smears across his face.

'That man is not fit to be let out by himself.' murmured Doc Holliday to Sludge who had the feeling that the fascination he was feeling at the unfolding demise of Ronan Coyne was akin to that experienced by observers at a public hanging.

'Who wants to come with me?' repeated Ronan. 'Ah, good,' he said as he saw a raised hand, 'at least there will be two of us.' he said with an air of defiance that quickly faded when he realised that the raised hand belonged to a smiling young man wearing a green Barbour jacket whose smile held no humour at all. 'On second thoughts,' said Ronan hastily, 'perhaps the idea of visiting the pub is a good idea, and we can go to 55 Kings Bench Street afterwards.'

'Wherever you are going, Dr Coyne,' said Mr Barbour walking forward, 'you are in obvious difficulties. I'll help you.' he said, ignoring Ronan's protests with an apparently good-natured smile. 'Place your right arm around my shoulders,' he instructed, that's right,' he said, gripping Ronan's wrist with his right hand as it came over his shoulder and placing his left arm his round Ronan's waist. 'We're ready for anything,' he said with a cheerfulness that almost everyone found reassuring, 'whoever is leading, lead on. We will bring up the rear. Don't worry about us, we'll be fine.' He turned to look at Ronan whose face was no more than six inches from his own, 'We will, won't we Dr Coyne?' he said. Miserable, tattered, blood streaked and spattered with gore, Ronan didn't reply.

Such is the frailty of human spirit that any feelings of disloyalty that might have been harboured for the unfortunate Ronan Coyne, were rapidly overcome by the prospect of a picnic, where once 'the poet had supped'. It has to be said that the emergence as leaders of Beryl and Joan, with their intimate knowledge of Albert Bleaney and their readiness to share their fund of stories about him, gave the walkers a keener sense of participation than the arid featureless trek that had begun under Ronan.

Most of the small band avoided his eye as they set off for the nearby Lady le Gros.

The cold-eyed man looked across at the odd couple. He knew that the younger man was very dangerous. The little foolish guy was in a bad way, but what did the other want with him? It was a puzzle and he felt that whatever the answer, it would favour the helper rather than the helped.

'Are you sure that you can manage?' Sludge and Doc Holliday were a couple of paces behind the band as they moved away and Sludge paused to ask the question of Ronan.

An unsmiling Mr Barbour glanced briefly at Sludge before looking over Ronan's head in the direction of the group from which the sound of animated chattering could now be heard.

'Ronan?' said Sludge.

Ronan Coyne lifted his head and stared at Sludge for several seconds before he hissed, 'Push off Ludgeworth, you've done enough damage for today.'

Sludge held Ronan's stare, then shrugged his shoulders and walked towards the edge of the clearing to join Doc Holliday who was gazing intently at Mr Barbour. Both men then turned to follow the main group who were heading for Top Path before crossing a field known locally as Corpo Field to walk alongside the Beck for a couple of hundred yards to where it adjoined the garden of the Lady le Gros.

Betty Turnbull was not the only member of the group who looked doubtfully at the stile leading from Top Path into a field. 'Oh dear,' she said, 'this is turning into quite an adventure. I'm tired. We've been walking a long time. I'm not quite sure…' her voice trailed off as she watched the much older (and thinner) Elsie Battle negotiate the obstacle without hesitation.

'Allow me, my dear,' Meredith Winstanley stepped forward, 'first we'll put these here,' he relieved Betty of the several bags she felt necessary to take with her everywhere she went, and placed them on the floor. 'Now, put your foot on the bottom step,' he gripped her wrist with one hand and her upper arm with the other, 'I'll keep you safe,' he said confidently, 'you won't fall.' Betty, who still hadn't quite recovered from the sensation of Ronan's leg quivering under her fingers, was emboldened by Meredith's firm grasp and cleared the stile with some speed, to stand on the other side breathless and slightly flushed as her bags were returned to her.

The small band surveyed the field in front of them, it declined gently to the Beck and looking to the right, they could see the outline of the Lady le Gros, clearly visible through a thin belt of trees.

'Ah, Miss Sanderson,' the Reverend Meadows addressed Joan, 'if you don't mind me asking, did you and Albert ever come this way?'

'Please, call me Joan,' she smiled, 'Yes, we did, but Beryl knows more about Corpo Field than I do. Beryl?' she looked enquiringly at her friend.

Joan and Beryl were enjoying themselves. Neither of them found any hardship in talking about Albert Bleaney the man, rather than the famous poet, to people who were anxious for any information, and who treated them with an almost reverential respect. Neither did they know that within two years they would become almost as well known as the poet himself.

Beryl took up the story. 'Albert used to play cricket on here,' she gestured at the field, 'when he was a boy. I remember him telling me about a particular game in which a boy called Johnnie Steen scored over one hundred runs, but took all day doing it. The other boys were very angry that they didn't have a chance to bat, so they set about poor Johnnie and finished up by throwing him into the Beck. Albert always said that that was a prime example of the English desire to pour scorn on sporting success.'

'Why is it called Corpo Field?' asked Elsie Battle, her pen poised above her notebook.

'I don't know.' said Beryl, 'Do you?' she turned to Joan.

'Just a minute.' said Joan, as a helicopter passed low overhead. 'Well, according to a story told to me by Albert, this field was once owned by a fat Conservative MP called Lord Corpulent, and Corpulent's Field eventually became known as Corpo Field.' Amid a gentle ripple of laughter she said, 'But I don't think that is very likely'

'What could be more English than this?' Doc Holliday, who with Sludge was still on the Top Path, was leaning on the stile looking down the field. 'Surrounded by hedges and trees, a stile, a meadow with little yellow flowers leading to a stream and an old pub in this distance.' The laughter from the group drifted up, 'They're having a good time.' he said.

Sludge glanced over Doc Holliday's shoulder and smiled before turning back to look down the path which ran straight for about a hundred yards before bending away to the left. 'No sign of them.' he said. They had realised that Ronan would need more than the help of Mr Barbour to negotiate the stile and had decided to hang back to offer assistance. Even allowing for the very slow pace the pair would be making, Sludge felt that they should have been in sight several minutes ago.

'Let's check them out.' said Doc Holliday; leaving the stile, he immediately set off down the path with a purposeful stride. The path was still clear when they rounded the bend and they were almost back at the site of Albert Bleaney's grave when, on turning a sharp corner, a disturbing sight greeted them. Some fifty yards distant, the young man in the green Barbour jacket was leaning against a tree. Opposite him, in the middle of the path, Ronan Coyne was lying on the ground. He wasn't moving.

The cold-eyed man froze. This looked bad. Very bad.

Doc Holliday walked up to the young man, 'Anything we can do?' he said, nodding at the inert figure.

'I doubt it,' said the young man evenly, 'I think the poor chap's had a heart attack. I've sent for the emergency services,' he held up a mobile telephone, 'they will be here shortly. They're sending an air ambulance.'

Sludge had approached the scene slowly and was now standing a few yards away. He thought how very small

Ronan was, and how stupid he looked lying there, no he corrected himself, not stupid, so very undignified.

'How will they know where we are?' he asked, unable to think of anything else to say.

'Because the phone he is using,' said Doc Holliday, 'is probably equipped with GSP.' He looked at the young man who offered no acknowledgement either of the assertion or the question in the look. 'I'm a doctor,' he said, not taking his eyes of Mr Barbour, 'I'll take a look at him.'

'A doctor of what?' said the young man, raising an eyebrow.

Ignoring the question, Doc Holliday, bending down onto one knee placed his fingers at the side of Ronan's throat; he left them there for a few seconds before moving them higher, and then lower. He gripped Ronan's chin and gently moved it, first to the left, then to the right, and then back again. He stood up and stepped back as two men wearing dark blue overalls appeared; they were running and carrying a stretcher.

The men glanced briefly at the tableau in front of them before, without saying a word, they set about securing Ronan to the stretcher. As they stood up, the stretcher between them, one man addressed Mr Barbour, 'You are to come with us.' Without waiting for an answer, they moved off at a brisk pace, the young man in the green Barbour jacket following closely behind them.

Stunned by the speed and sequence of events Sludge sat on the ground, his back against a tree, staring down the path. It was only after a helicopter passed low overhead that Doc Holliday broke the silence.

'Billy,' he said, 'listen to me, this is very important. Tell me everything you know about that young man.' He looked at Sludge, who continued to stare down the path. 'Billy, listen to me,' he insisted, 'Ronan Coyne is dead. I think that his neck had been broken.'

TEN

Sludge spends an evening at home

'Yes, Vice Chancellor, I'll be there, ten o'clock, in your room.' Sludge was speaking on the telephone to Professor Badowski about the arrangements for the lifting of his suspension. 'Yes,' he said after listening to Badowski explaining somewhat enigmatically how it was time for everyone to pull together, 'I appreciate that very much. Goodbye, I'll see you in the morning, goodbye.' He put down the telephone and crossed to the window to look over the park. It was late afternoon on the day following the inaugural Albert Bleaney Walk. Led by Joan and Beryl, it seemed the walk had been a huge success. One or two tentative polite enquiries were made concerning the whereabouts and state of health of Ronan Coyne, but they had been deflected without difficulty by vague references to Mr Barbour having taken him home.

Sludge had invited Doc Holliday back to his flat after the conclusion of the walk and had recounted, in as much detail as he could remember, his encounters with Mr Barbour. He had also showed him the pubic hair and flower petals. Although he crudely referred to the find as the 'pubes and petals', Doc Holliday showed great interest, both in that, and in the series of clues that had led to Sludge's forthcoming meeting with the London solicitors. It was quite late when he left Sludge; and only after he had made several unsuccessful calls trying to establish which hospital had admitted Ronan Coyne.

Against Doc Holliday's advice, who thought it a useless exercise, Sludge telephoned the central police station in Kingston. He told them that Ronan had apparently had a heart attack and had been airlifted to an unknown hospital. The police were sympathetic and promised to help. Early on Sunday morning Sludge received a telephone call confirming that Ronan Coyne had been admitted to York General Hospital, from where he had been transferred to a specialist unit. The caller, an apologetic youngish sounding woman, then expressed her regret in having to inform Sludge that Ronan Coyne had died during emergency surgery following a massive heart attack. As Doc Holliday had suggested, the story was solid enough, and although it had the flavour of a cover up, it would be, he had also suggested, impossible to prove that Ronan's death was anything other than a natural one.

The helplessness that Sludge had experienced when faced with the implacable force of the American authorities overwhelmed him once more. He stared out at the trees, but the image in his mind was of the crumpled inert figure of Ronan Coyne lying on the cemetery path. He really disliked the man, but, he thought, even he deserved better than a grubby end at the hands of a state sponsored psychopath.

Directly opposite Sludge's window stood a magnificent horse chestnut tree. He opened the window wide and addressed the tree in a very loud voice, 'Any man's death diminishes me, because I am involved in mankind; and therefore never send to know for whom the bells tolls; it tolls for thee.' The reverberations of his voice hung in the silence; then, from the other side of the park came the sound of church bells, calling worshippers to evensong. Sludge heard the sound and shrugged his shoulders, 'It tolls for thee,' he said softly, 'it tolls for thee'.

The cold-eyed man examined his packet of cigarettes. Two left, he noted that he was smoking more heavily than usual. He was worried about the kid. The death of the funny little guy had got to him. Among other things, the sight of the body had made him realise that he couldn't kill Poisonous Pete. He never could of course. The cold-eyed man blew cigarette smoke through the open window and watched it swirl away in the light breeze. The kid wasn't a killer. Never would be.

Somebody Up There Likes You

On the reasonable grounds that the first girl to touch his penis was from Liverpool, and who only consented to sleep with Sludge if he agreed to pretend to be Kenny Dalglish (Liverpool FC's captain at the time), Sludge had been a keen supporter of the Liverpool football team. To his regret, he had never visited the Anfield ground in Liverpool, but he had watched the team on the numerous occasions their matches were televised. For many years he had been puzzled why the Liverpool supporters apparently chanted 'the mon-key men' in support of their team. It was only when he told Sheila about this oddity that she had, between fits of giggles, explained that the crowd were in fact exhorting 'come on you reds'.

So it was that, when Sludge was cycling towards the University on Monday morning having received a telephone call from a nervous sounding Vice Chancellor Badowski asking him to come in immediately, to, 'quell this - ah - disturbance', and he heard a distant chant of 'kill Betty Black' repeated over and over, he decided not to trust his ears.

Standing astride his bicycle in the middle of the road, waiting for a break in the traffic heading into town so that he could turn right into the University, Sludge looked across at the hundred or so students gathered just inside the campus gates. It was this group who were chanting. Sludge realised that they intended no harm to the mysterious 'Betty Black', but were in fact calling 'let Billy back'. He saw that some of the protesters were holding hastily prepared banners announcing, among other things, 'Free The East Riding One', 'Billy is Innocent', and somewhat strangely, held by Fabio Brindisi he noticed, 'I've Walked Down The Boulevard of Broken Dreams'.

A huge cheer greeted him as the students saw him ride slowly into the campus. Quite overwhelmed by the reception, Sludge dismounted, and holding the handlebars of his bicycle, faced the exhilarated throng as the cheers gave way to renewed shouts of 'bring Billy back', accompanied by rhythmic clapping, stamping, and waving of banners. Sludge looked at the laughing, excited faces of the students, and suddenly, with an almost physical jolt, his inward eye saw the sullen, threatening faces of the National Guard lined up against them. Someone began to sing 'You'll Never Walk Alone', a song that was quickly taken up by everyone. Completely at a loss, Sludge raised his hand, the singing gradually subsided, and then stopped altogether; leaving a complete silence as the protesters looked expectantly at the solitary figure standing in front of them; his familiar Stetson shading his eyes and his long black jacket unfastened and blowing open in the gentle breeze. The silence stretched to the point of becoming uncomfortable when a voice called out, 'What's happening Billy?' An appreciative murmur accompanied this call as Sludge looked at the speaker and beckoned him forward. Danny Graziano moved to the front row of the students and nodded at Sludge.

'Danny,' said Sludge, struggling to keep his voice under control, 'please, ask everyone to leave.'

'No deal, Billy,' said Danny Graziano, 'we are here to make sure you come back'. A cheer greeted this comment as the student moved forward and looked into Sludge's eyes. 'We need you man.' he said.

Sludge swallowed hard. 'I'm here to see the VC.' he said. He looked across at the students, 'I will see the VC and then tell everyone what is happening. I will be in the main lecture theatre at 11.00 o'clock to talk to all who are interested. Please tell them that.'

'You're on Billy.' the young man grinned, and held his hand out to Sludge who shook it, thereby heralding another enormous cheer.

Looking down on the scene from his third floor room in the Administration Block, Vice Chancellor Badowski was holding a letter in his hand as he watched Sludge slowly wheel his bicycle through the cheering mass of students, his progress hampered by many handshakes and pats on the back. He continued to watch after Sludge had passed out of sight and was relieved to see that after one of the group had briefly addressed them, the protesters began to drift away from the campus gates.

Badowski turned to Dean Croucher with whom he had been discussing the letter he held, 'Ludgeworth's courses are the most demanding in the University and his academic standards most rigorous, and yet his popularity with the students is plain to see.' he said. 'What does that tell you about the student body?' he asked, raising his bushy eyebrows so that they merged into his drooping forelock thereby accentuating the impression that he was staring through almost impenetrable foliage. Dean Croucher, hoping that the question was rhetorical, smiled weakly in silent reply. After staring at her for what seemed several minutes, he continued, 'The circumstances by which we can bring him back are as fortuitous as they are mysterious, but in view of this,' he brandished the letter he was holding, 'we should be grateful.'

The letter, which had been delivered by hand that morning was from Dr Peter Pelham announcing his immediate resignation. He gave no explanation other than to declare that he was 'leaving the area immediately for personal reasons'. He also made clear that he would not return, left instructions for any monies to be paid into his bank, and donated the contents of his room to Dr William Ludgeworth, 'to do with as he thinks fit'. Dean Croucher, who had answered the urgent summons to Badowski's room believing that they were to discuss Sludge's reinstatement, was dumbfounded to be confronted with the news about Pelham's abrupt departure. At Badowski's request, she had read the letter, and apart from being able to confirm Pelham's handwriting, was unable to shed any light on the suddenness of his departure. Neither could she offer any explanation as to why he should leave anything at all to Sludge, unless it was 'some sort of joke'.

As Pelham's telephone appeared to have been disconnected and his mobile number was unobtainable, it was suggested by Dean Croucher that she contact her sister, who lived only a mile or so from Pelham's flat, to check if he was there. Very pleased to have a chance for some excitement, Serena Croucher had jumped at the opportunity. Twenty minutes later she had telephoned to confirm that the flat was deserted and to offer the extra information that, according to a neighbour, Pelham had left yesterday in the late morning. He was in the company of a youngish man wearing a short red windcheater-type jacket and blue jeans. Some suitcases and boxes had been loaded into a white van that was driven away by the young man. The neighbour confirmed that Pelham was in the passenger seat, and thought that another man, as well as the driver, was there. And that appeared to be that. Pelham had resigned, had left the district and apparently had no intention of coming back.

Badowski was in a dilemma, on the one hand, he was glad to see Pelham go as he considered him to be a quite awful man. He didn't believe the accusations levelled by Sludge; there was after all no evidence. But Pelham did appear to be an amoral man whose chief assets were manipulation and low cunning. On the other hand, his 'disappearance' was out of character and he thought very briefly about informing the police, before deciding that he would accept the letter at face value and get on with the day-to-day business of running the university.

'Ludgeworth will be here shortly, Desiree.' Badowski said, as he moved to sit behind his desk. 'I'll ask him to come and see you,' he paused and smiled before adding, 'it will be up to you to see if he is prepared to offer any help in view of Pelham's departure.' Desiree Croucher nodded somewhat distractedly and left the room as Badowski began to reread Pelham's letter, shaking his head and muttering as he did so.

At that moment Sludge was alone in a small room reserved for private study at the back of the library. He had chosen this room because he didn't want to be disturbed and he needed to compose himself before the meeting with Badowski. The demonstration that had greeted him a few minutes earlier had disturbed him. Of course, the sudden flashback to the actions of the National Guard on that awful day in Texas twenty years ago was very unsettling, but he knew it was more than a bad memory. It was the sudden realisation, or perhaps the confirmation of something he had known, but had resisted knowing, that for him little had changed since that catastrophe. He was still the student's friend, and was still going nowhere, he thought without self-pity or rancour.

Sitting in that quiet room random images filled his mind: he heard Sheila's voice crying, 'Hello there, Billy Sludge'; saw Birdy Kaplanski lying in a hospital bed, pale faced and with dried blood in her hair; saw Ronan Coyne's lifeless body; and saw himself as a young boy in a comfortable, firelit room with his brother and his parents, his father listening to the radio with his two sons, his mother knitting. Sludge leaned back with closed eyes and tried to hear the radio, but instead other images intruded. He saw pictures of places that had long since vanished: his first school, the house where he was born, both flattened in Government sponsored clearance schemes, his Grammar school was also no longer there, neither were any of the streets where he had played with his friends. His friends, he thought, where were they? These absences fed in to the sense of disconnection and dislocation he had become aware of after the death of his parents. It seemed that, without his being aware of it, they had anchored him into a comfortable melancholia that was his past. Now he had no anchor. He saw himself drifting in space, turning slowly, head over heels, and going nowhere. The black dog began to gnaw at his stomach as Sludge slumped forward with his head on the table.

The cold-eyed man drew deeply on his cigarette. Unashamedly he flicked a tear from his cheek. He sighed heavily and tilted his chair onto its back legs, resting his head and shoulders against the wall as he did so. He had no water, no food, and in front of him stretched the parched desert and in the distance, the mountains. And beyond that, who knows? Standing up with another heavy sigh the cold-eyed man fastened his jacket, replaced his hat and left the room.

'It appears that you know some very powerful people, Billy'. Badowski said, in such a way that the statement was also a question. He looked at Sludge who was sitting on his hands, his shoulders hunched and his head bowed. He had not reacted as Badowski had anticipated. In fact he had not reacted at all other than a humourless - embarrassed almost - half grin and a slight shrug of the shoulders at the news that the police had no intention of pursuing a possible prosecution; and further, that the good people of Shrivellsea had unreservedly withdrawn their complaints. Therefore, there were no grounds on which the University could consider any action other than the immediate withdrawal of his suspension. 'Very powerful indeed.' said Badowski quietly, almost to himself.

Apparently, the Chief Constable of the East Riding had telephoned the Chairman of the Governors to tell them of the decision to drop any interest in Sludge, and had suggested, informally of course, but with some force, that the University take a lenient view of the 'minor transgression'. He also revealed the incredible news that the prostitutes had, *en masse* as it were, suddenly left Shrivellsea. In addition, an anonymous donor had made a very acceptable donation to the development fund of the Shrivellsea Community Centre. It was implied that anything other than a complete withdrawal of threatened action against Sludge would severely jeopardise the benefits to Shrivellsea as well as heralding other 'unwanted complications'.

'Yes,' murmured Badowski, looking for some reaction from a strangely subdued Sludge, 'powerful, powerful people.'

Sludge stood up, 'I'm very grateful to you, Vice Chancellor,' he said, 'but now I would like to go and get on with my work.'

'Before you go, Billy,' Badowski picked up Pelham's letter from his desk and handed it across to Sludge, saying as he did so, 'you should read this, I'm sure you will find it of interest.

Sludge remained standing as he took the letter from Badowski's hand and, out of habit, looked first at the signature. Surprised, he glanced up briefly, and then read the letter through once, and then again, before looking enquiringly at the Vice Chancellor.

'If that look is your way of asking for an explanation, Billy I have none. Pelham has resigned with immediate effect. Evidently, it is as simple as that, unless of course you have heard something?'

Slowly, Sludge shook his head, thinking of the conversation with Doc Holliday in the Empire Tea Rooms. He was aware that he did know something, but he wasn't sure what that something was, 'No,' he said wearily, 'nothing. What could I know? I've been suspended.'

Badowski smiled as he retrieved the letter from Sludge, 'Well yes, of course,' he said, 'Pelham's sudden departure leaves us with the immediate problem of covering his classes. If you can help Dean Croucher, I'm sure she would appreciate that.'

'I'm sure she would,' said Sludge, 'I'll talk to her. OK if I go now?'

Badowski nodded, and for a few seconds stared at the door that Sludge had closed behind him, before he rose from his desk and walked to the window, where he stood, hands behind his back, looking blindly at the campus while humming tunelessly.

Sludge paused in the outer office to Badowski's room and looked at the Vice Chancellor's secretary who stopped typing and returned his gaze. Veronica, who was within a year or so of retirement, hadn't worked anywhere else and was well used to the tortuous machinations of life at the University. Nevertheless, she had found recent events, Sludge's suspension, and then Pelham's resignation, to be disturbing.

'Veronica,' he said, 'are you still connected with fund raising for the RSPCA?'

'I am.' said Veronica, puzzled.

'Of course, you know that Pelham has resigned.' he said.

Veronica nodded warily, she knew the matter was confidential, but accepted that the news was probably all round the campus by now.

'I'm sure that the VC will give you the details, but, for whatever reason, Pelham has given me the contents of his room. In my turn I would like to give them to you, to do with as you think fit. I'm sure that his books at least will be worth something. Are you interested?'

Veronica smiled and nodded. 'The RSPCA is an appropriate choice.' she said, recalling the time when a large friendly dog had adopted the campus as its home. There had been no trouble at all until the dog came across Peter Pelham and had promptly bitten him.

'That's settled then.' Sludge said. At the door he turned and added, 'By the way I will be off campus on Wednesday, I'm taking a day's leave.'

Sludge left the Administration Building through a little used side door and walked around the back of the campus, before entering Carter Hall through the deserted Caretaker's Office, so that he could approach his room via the emergency stairs. He was avoiding contact with anyone because he needed time to think. Glancing at his watch, he saw that it was ten twenty; he had forty minutes before he was due to address the students as promised.

The cold-eyed man looked out warily from the head of the stairs, his hand on his revolver. He saw the corridor was empty and grunted with satisfaction. Gliding swiftly and stealthily, he reached the room and quickly entered, to stand with his back against the door as it closed noiselessly behind him. He glanced around the familiar room; when he left, only a few days ago - although it seemed longer - he wasn't sure that he would see it again. Now the kid was back - as if nothing had changed. There had been changes. The little guy was dead, murdered probably, and Poisonous Pete had resigned. The resignation was unlikely, he mused, blowing a stream of blue smoke at the ceiling. Doc Holliday had asked questions about Poisonous Pete and had mentioned the girl from Madrid. Now Poisonous Pete had disappeared. The cold-eyed man knew that the Doc was a friend of the kid. But he was also a dangerous man with obvious access to powerful people. He narrowed his eyes against the drifting cigarette smoke. Was the Doc a puppet-master, or merely a puppet, he pondered. With finger and thumb he squeezed the burning end off his cigarette, dropping the glowing ember to the floor where he crushed it underfoot. Putting the unsmoked butt behind his ear he sat at the desk and leaning back in the chair propped his booted feet on the desk. Whoever the Doc was, the cold-eyed man considered, whoever he was connected with, the kid had no option but to ride with him for a few more miles. He owed him that.

Sludge took off his hat and laid it on the table, then walked across to the podium and placed a book on the lectern. Taking up a position behind the lectern, his hands resting lightly on the sides, he looked at his audience. The Florence M Atkinson Lecture Theatre held three hundred people and was almost full. In the front row he could see Fabio Brindisi anxiously scanning the notes Sludge had handed to him moments before, notes that gave specific instructions and advice on what he needed to do to retrieve his failed paper and to secure a pass. Sitting here and there in isolated pockets of space, Sludge was surprised to see some of his colleagues. The lecture theatre was steeply raked and glancing up he saw Dean Croucher sitting on the very back row. Just in front of her and to the right he spotted Doc Holliday. Further to the right, he noticed a dark haired young woman, lightly tanned and wearing a bright yellow sweater, although she smiled encouragingly at him and moved her hand in a shy little wave, he was fairly certain he had never seen her before.

Tumultuous applause, which he had acknowledged with a slight inclination of his head, had greeted his entrance. The wild clapping and cheering had continued for a minute or so as Sludge made his preparations. The overwhelming noise gradually subsided into an animated buzz that faded as Sludge continued to look around the audience. The lecture hall was completely silent as he moved the microphone nearer to him, picked up the book and slowly turned the pages.

'This is the final paragraph from *In Dubious Battle*, by John Steinbeck.' he said quietly, his amplified voice filling the auditorium. Several members of the audience exchanged knowing glances. Sludge often began his lectures by reading from a prepared text, sometimes a poem, sometimes a song lyric, sometimes from a work of fiction. A by-product of this practice, of which he may well have been unaware, was his habit of adopting an approximation of the speaking voice of the writer. Thus, for example, he read Sylvia Plath in harsh New England tones, Philip Larkin's voice was plummy, middle England and middle class, and Dambudzo Marechera had the rounded mellifluous ring of central Southern Africa combined with the edge of an exaggerated 'English' pronunciation. He never explained himself and the link to his topic was seldom, if ever, immediately obvious, but for those who bothered to look, it was always there to be found.

'London handed the lantern up,' he read out in a soft Californian drawl, 'and Mac set it carefully on the floor, beside the body, so that its light fell on the head. He stood up and faced the crowd. His hands gripped the rail. His eyes were wide and white. In front he could see the massed men, eyes shining in the lamplight. Behind the front row, the men were lumped and dark. Mac shivered. He moved his jaws to speak, and it seemed to break the frozen jaws loose. His voice was high and monotonous. 'This guy didn't want for nothing himself - ' he began. His knuckles were white, where he grasped the rail. 'Comrades! He didn't want nothing for himself-'.'

Sludge turned the page and stared down at the closed book before he lifted his head, squared his shoulders, and looked into the body of the hall.

The University accused me of various offences.' he said. 'I was accused of gross misconduct.' He paused and felt the electric edge of the audience's anticipation surge through him, 'I was accused of bringing the name of the University into disrepute.' He paused again. 'I was accused of behaving foolishly and discreditably.' Noises from outside the lecture theatre emphasised the stillness within. Sludge lowered his eyes as if in contemplation, before lifting his head with a sharp movement and declaring, 'I stand guilty as charged. I expect to be punished. I deserve to be punished.'

Sludge gripped the lectern tightly as low mumbles from the audience filled the silence that followed his words. Spellbound by the sense of theatre Sludge had generated Dean Croucher regarded the scene with some apprehension, and wondered if she was about to witness a very public resignation.

'And yet,' said Sludge, with a dramatic emphasis that once more brought about complete silence, 'although I am guilty, I am not to be punished.' Cheers that were quickly stifled greeted this announcement as it became clear to the audience from Sludge's attitude that he was not making a valedictory speech.

'I am grateful to you,' he gestured at the audience, 'for your support,' he held up his hand at the ripple of applause, 'but it made no difference. My fate had already been decided; decided by people, unknown to you, but also and more importantly, unknown to me.' He paused. 'That isn't quite true,' he said, looking at Doc Holliday who, captivated by the theatricality of the performance and ignoring the sidelong glances from those around him, touched the brim of his hat in acknowledgement as Sludge continued, 'I do know something of one of the foot soldiers, but nothing of the officers, or indeed of what army he represents.'

'Many years ago,' Sludge went on, 'on a sunny day in Texas, I stood in a line such as the one you formed this morning. As a result of my involvement, I was deported from the land of the free, and told never to go back. I never met the decision makers. I was simply moved from A to B by their actions. On that sunny day in Texas, people were damaged, physically and psychologically, and it was all to no avail. Nothing changed. The grey people, the suits, won; they did so without showing their faces, without raising a sweat.' Sludge almost whispered into the microphone, 'Nothing changed.' as an image of the pale and bloodied Birdy Kaplanski flashed across his consciousness.

'Nothing changed.' He repeated, gripping the sides of the lectern so that his knuckles shone through the stretched skin.

'I had a meeting with the Vice Chancellor this morning.' he said, only just controlling his impulse to parody Neville Chamberlain's, 'I had a meeting with Herr Hitler' address. 'Once more, unknown people have made life-changing decisions about me, this time to my benefit, it would seem. But is it?' he asked rhetorically, raising his shoulders and looking up at Dean Croucher.

Suddenly Sludge felt very weary. He abandoned his plan to discuss the desirability of individual sovereignty in confronting anonymous corporate powerbrokers, and decided to bring his presentation to a speedy end.

'I am not leaving the University.' he said. 'I am staying until the end of this semester and, as I have decided that I do want something for myself, I will then spend some time deciding what to do with the rest of my life. As for you lot,' he managed to grin at the audience, 'I suggest that you do the same.'

To the accompaniment of a storm of clapping, stamping and cheering, Sludge left the podium and picked up his hat from the nearby table; lifting the hat high he acknowledged the acclamation, and quickly took his leave. Anxious to speak to Sludge, Dean Croucher also left the building with some haste. Using the emergency exit, she appeared at the top of the fire escape in time to see Sludge emerge below her.

On hearing his name called out from somewhere above his head, Sludge had been somewhat alarmed to see the bulky Dean, skirts billowing, clattering down the iron stairs with little apparent regard for either decorum or safety. He had a sudden inward vision of the Dean lying at the bottom of the stairs with himself called upon to administer first aid, 'Take it easy Desiree,' he called urgently, 'take it easy.' Given impetus by her weight and the rake of the stairs, Dean Croucher negotiated the final half dozen steps in two enormous strides. Stepping neatly to one side, Sludge watched in quiet amazement as Dean Croucher, arms flailing, hurtled past him to disappear round the side of the building. He walked to the corner and peeped around. Crimson faced, Dean Croucher was leaning against the wall with both hands to her breasts, which were heaving up and down like a wild animal caught in a net.

Tuning her head, she saw Sludge, 'Billy,' she gasped, 'we've got to talk.'

'Take it easy, Desiree,' he said again, 'I'm not going anywhere.' He moved to stand alongside the Dean. 'Let's sit down' he said pointing. Placing a hand under her elbow, Sludge guided Desiree to a nearby bench, where they sat quietly, watching the students as they made their way across the campus towards the refectory. He saw Doc Holliday turn off the path and walk across towards him.

'Sorry to disturb you.' he said. Lifting his hat, he smiled at Dean Croucher, before addressing Sludge, 'I'm going for a coffee with your friend Fabio - perhaps you will join us when you're through here?'

'Perhaps.' said Billy.

Doc Holliday smiled again, 'Beware the lady in yellow, Billy.' he said, and then nodded to the Dean and walked off to rejoin Fabio Brindisi who had been standing awkwardly alone a short distance away. Just beyond him the young woman in the bright yellow sweater was talking in animated fashion to Danny Graziano, who was staring intently at the ground as they walked slowly a few paces behind a group of students.

'Are you leaving us, Billy?' said Dean Croucher staring at the retreating Doc Holliday.

'Maybe, maybe not,' he said, 'but if I do decide to go, I will give you plenty of notice, unlike the ever reliable and dependable Dr Pelham.'

Dean Croucher swallowed hard and ignored the heavy sarcasm, 'Yes,' she murmured, 'his sudden decision has left us with a mess to sort out. Can you help?'

'By taking over some of his teaching, I suppose,' he said, looking at the Dean who simply nodded. 'I'm sorry Desiree,' he said, 'but I just don't have the time.' Or the inclination, he thought to himself. 'Ask a part-timer. I'm sure Mr do-anything-anywhere-anytime would be only too happy to oblige.'

'You mean Bill Penny, I presume.' Desiree said with a half smile, 'I'm sure that he would.'

Although Dean Croucher had a well-deserved reputation for often extreme expediency in getting a job done, she was against the ever increasing use of part time staff working on short term, temporary contracts. She was, of course, aware of the strong economic argument for a flexible workforce where the resource could be turned on or off according to demand. But her experience showed her that if the employer didn't offer loyalty and commitment, then the employee was no more than a mercenary. And, that being the case, if they adopted the morals of a mercenary, who could blame them? Bill Penny was a case in point; he was a clever man who always worked to his own agenda and who considered that the only worthwhile point of a system or procedure was one that could be subverted to his own advantage. She could never actually establish that he was responsible for the minor disasters that lurked around the fringes of everything he touched, in any case he always provided a hint of where she could find someone more culpable than him, to the extent that her private name for him was 'Bill the Betrayer'.

'Yes, Bill Penny,' she said half to herself, 'we're in trouble, Billy,' she said with resolve and then surprised her listener by adding, 'but not that much. We'll get by without the likes of Bill Penny.'

There was a lot Dean Croucher wanted to know from Sludge. Who was the American with the hat and the moustache? Was he involved in Sludge's reprieve? Did he have a theory on Pelham's disappearance? What about this chap who had had a heart attack, how was Sludge involved in that? Why should he beware the lady in yellow? Although she was anxious for information, she knew from his general demeanour that this was not the time to ask questions.

'Help me up, Billy,' she said shuffling forward on the seat, 'these benches were designed for skinny students not academics of more mature years.' Sludge stood up and held Dean Croucher's arm while she levered herself into an upright position and managed to stand.

'Thanks, Billy,' she said, 'are you heading my way?' she nodded in the direction of Burbanks Hall.

Sludge shook his head, 'No,' he said, 'I need a word with my friend from Colorado, and then I must get down to some work. Oh, by the way,' he said, as he turned to head for the refectory, 'I am taking a day's leave on Wednesday.'

Dean Croucher opened her mouth to ask who had authorised his absence, but once more Sludge's manner deterred her. The astute observer would have noticed the Dean's lips moving as she strolled towards Burbanks Hall. 'Pelham gone, Billy Sludge on the edge, mysterious Americans and sudden deaths, these are strange and troubling times,' she muttered, 'strange and troubling times.'

ELEVEN

They're Back!

It was early in the evening when Sludge left the University and decided to cycle home via the park opposite his flat. He watched the swifts spiralling overhead as he wheeled his cycle between the horse chestnut trees, and walked across to the small lake that he could glimpse from his high window. The lake was fringed with large rocks, worn smooth by one and a half centuries and the backsides of countless small boys, who, even in this age of 'home based entertainment', could, on occasion, still be seen fishing for sticklebacks or 'taddies'.

The park was almost deserted. It was that awkward time; too late for children and parents, and too early for those who needed darkness to cloak their activities. Sludge lay his cycle on the grass and walked slowly to the water's edge where he sat on a rock to watch the swifts chasing each other across the surface. He remembered how Sheila was always the first to spot the return of the migrating swifts in mid April, 'They're back.' she would cry exultantly. He also remembered that he was always the one to notice that they had left as summer drew to a close. The swifts extended their chasing game to swoop around Sludge, screaming as they did so. Above the screams, Sludge heard Sheila's voice cry, 'they're back,' and he realised that he was weeping.

The cold-eyed man stiffened. A flash of bright yellow between the trees signalled he was not alone. Shading his eyes, he saw the young woman who had waved to the kid. The woman in yellow. She was coming this way. Maybe she was just passing through.

Sludge removed his hat and balanced it on his crooked knee while rubbing both hands vigorously about his face in a rough washing motion. He replaced his hat and saw that the young woman in the bright yellow sweater was heading directly towards him, she smiled and waved when she realised he was looking at her and jogged across.

"Phew,' she said, her hand to her chest, 'I don't think I'm fit enough for such exertions. Hello, Dr Ludgeworth,' she said, 'I'm Ann Gora. Danny told me everyone calls you Billy Sludge, can I call you Billy, or would you prefer Dr Sludge?' she offered her hand and laughed.

Sludge took her hand while thinking that her voice sounded vaguely familiar, 'Dr Sludge will be fine.' he said, smiling, 'Tell me, what came first, the name or the sweater?'

'Yes,' she said, stroking the long woollen fibres of her sweater, 'it is a bit obvious I suppose. I used to wear a red weatherproof as Ann Orak, and for one very special job,' she assumed a mock serious expression, 'I was Norma Negligee. My department is obsessed with clothing,' she said cheerily, 'my boss is known as V C Crombie.'

'Crombie I understand, but why V C?' said Sludge.

'Velvet collared.' she replied, putting her hand to her mouth like a child caught in a naughty act.

Sludge regarded Ann Gora carefully as she grinned and sat down, leaning forward to trail her fingers in the water. He saw a vibrant, open and friendly young woman and decided to react to that, but also to keep Doc Holliday's warning in mind.

'Ann,' he said, 'I've had a difficult few days and I have no desire to increase those difficulties by playing word games with you. OK?' She nodded, a trace of a smile around her lips, her eyes cool and appraising.

'Will Mr Barbour be coming back?' Sludge said.

'No,' Ann Gora said, watching the swifts tumbling across the sky, 'he has been sent for retraining. He will then probably get a desk job for a year or so while he is reassessed.'

'Did he kill Ronan Coyne?'

'I don't know,' she said, brushing her wet fingertips together, 'he says not. Dr Coyne died of a heart attack; he also had a broken neck. The story is that he was running through the woods in an agitated state when he suffered a massive heart attack that caused him to keel over and break his neck. Officially the heart attack killed him - as I told you on Sunday morning.'

'Ah, yes,' said Sludge, 'the telephone call, I thought I recognised your voice.' Ann Gora turned her head and glanced sideways at him, although not conventionally pretty there was vitality and a naturalness about her that was very appealing thought Sludge. He stood up and retrieved his bicycle, 'Shall we walk around the lake?' he said.

'Good idea.' she responded. Sludge was not what she expected him to be at all. After attending Barbour's de-briefing, she had an impression that she would find a woolly minded, effete individual. Another Barbour mistake she thought, as such was obviously not the case,

Sludge's presentation had shown him to be a man of style and depth, thoughtful, sensitive and courageous, but he was also a man who was clearly very troubled. 'I've answered two questions, three if you count the invitation to walk around the lake.' she said, 'Can I ask a question now?'

The cold-eyed man caught his breath. The kid's defences were low. His hand hovered over the butt of his pistol.

'Depends what the question is.' said Sludge warily.

'My Granddad had a bike just like yours,' she said, 'can I have a ride please?'

Completely taken aback, Sludge laughed, and after a moments hesitation during which he decided not to reveal the identity of the original owner, proffered the bicycle across to her and inclined his head as he said, 'It will be my pleasure.'

With a gleeful whoop, the young woman hitched up her short black skirt, took the handlebars, walked down the path a few paces, and then stood on one pedal to push herself off. Swinging the other leg over she mounted Mr Bleaney's bike, and was soon pedalling around the grass, laughing with unfeigned delight. 'Do you fancy a ride on the crossbar'? she shouted, as she swerved onto the path and cut between Sludge and the lakeside.

Laughing, he shook his head as she stopped directly in front of him.

'How about I sit on the handlebars while you pedal, then?' she persisted.

'My Paul Newman to your Ali McGraw, you mean?'

'Exactly,' she said, 'you have the boots, the hat and the jacket, you really look the part. How about it Dr Sundance?'

Driving along Queen's Avenue on his way home after a prolonged meeting with Desiree Croucher, Professor Max Badowski glanced across the park on his left. In the distance he could see two figures on a bicycle, a young woman in a bright yellow sweater was sitting on the handlebars while the machine was being pedalled by a man wearing a black hat, his jacket streaming out behind him as the pair cut a figure of eight across the grass. 'Students,' he grinned to himself, 'don't you just love them.' He turned his gaze back to the main road, and, putting the cyclists from his mind, once more began to consider Dean Croucher's gloomy prognosis on Sludge's state of mind and intentions.

'My guess is that you've done that before.' said Ann Gora, standing in front of Sludge, her hands on her hips.

'You'd be right,' Sludge grinned awkwardly, 'as a matter of fact, right here,' he swept his arm around the immediate area, 'a different bike though'. Sitting on the bicycle with one foot on a pedal and the other on the ground he glanced around. His inner ear heard Sheila shouting over and over again 'Raindrops keep falling on my head', as she later explained, those were the only words to the song that she knew. They had circled round and round until they had fallen off, then lying on the ground, they had watched the swifts cavorting above them. Later they had shared a bottle of wine and pledged their futures together. 'Yes, I've done it before.' he said quietly.

'On a different bike?' she probed gently.

'The bike belonged to Sheila, she took it with her when she moved to Denmark. That was a few years ago, I was supposed to follow on, but' he shrugged his shoulders helplessly 'I didn't, and now, I think I've lost her.'

Ann Gora regarded the forlorn figure on the bicycle, saw his crestfallen face as he struggled to control his emotions, and did the only thing possible for her to do. She stepped forward and took him in her arms 'Oh, Billy,' she said, 'what a mess you've got yourself into.'

The cold-eyed man took his hand off the butt of his revolver and sighed. The kid was in trouble. If this was a game the woman in yellow was playing, she held all the cards. The kid was vulnerable.

Sludge allowed Ann to hold him for a while then moved out of her arms, laid the bicycle on the grass and walked across to sit near the lake. As she sat down next to him, he looked across at her and said, 'Ask your questions, Ann. Ask your questions.'

'My name is Ann, it is not Ann Gora, neither is it Ann Orak, but it is Ann.' she said, her voice low and clear. 'I am a civil servant and I work in a section within a section within another section that is part of a sub division of the Ministry of Defence. My section is concerned with matters of security affecting the state, and has specific responsibility for security issues that may affect the Royal Family. I assume that Barbour told you very little?' she said.

Sludge picked up a small pebble from near his feet and tossed it into the water. 'He told me that he was looking for something. He wouldn't say what it was, only that if I saw it I would know. And, apart from threatening me with violence, that was about the extent of our communication'. Sludge rooted among the stones at his feet and picked up a round black pebble and began turning it over in his fingers. 'Oh, yes,' he said, 'he broke two vases that had belonged to Albert Bleaney's mother. Nice chap.' he said, throwing the black pebble into the middle of the lake.

Ann watched the ripples spreading across the lake. 'Some years ago,' she said, 'there was a strong rumour that a member of the Royal Family was giving out souvenirs of an intimate and personal nature. I cannot name the royal involved, nor can I give details of the alleged gift. To do so, I am instructed, would lend credence to what, even after all this time, remains an unsubstantiated rumour.' She stood up and walked a few paces to retrieve a broken branch, about three feet long, that she hauled to the edge of the lake. Grasping the thin tapered end, she whirled it round her head twice before hurling it into the lake, where it landed with a tremendous splash. 'I hate peddling the party line but...' she left the sentence unfinished as she sat down again and stared at the ripples lapping across the water. 'I suppose that is what it's all about,' she said, 'someone or something makes a splash, and the ripples go on forever, or what seems like forever. And people like me spend time trying to make sure they don't cause repercussions by landing on the wrong shore.'

Sludge was aware that Ann hadn't said all she wanted to say, and decided to wait until she broke the silence, which was stretching into minutes. While still staring at the water she said quietly, 'We have the names of those who may well have received such a royal souvenir. Albert Bleaney is on the list, and, it is fairly certain, that if he was so honoured then the personal gift was presented to him on the seventeenth of July 1985, shortly after he collected his OBE.'

The cold-eyed man froze on hearing these words. The kid had the goods. No doubt about that now. Albert Bleaney had been involved with someone from the Royal Family. Great care was needed. The kid had to keep a cool head.

'You said 'the wrong shore'', Sludge said, 'ripples on the wrong shore. Who decides whether a shore is right or wrong, you?'

'Not me,' Ann said slowly, shaking her head from side to side, 'not me.'

Sludge placed his hands, fingers laced, under his knee and gently pulled it towards his chest, 'So,' he said, 'when you find, if you find, one of these 'personal souvenirs' you will hand it over, and move on to the next job?'

Ann looked at him sharply, 'Make your point.' she said.

'Make my point?' Sludge said, taken aback by the edge in her voice. 'I'm not trying to make a point. Barbour barged into my life bringing alarm, despondency and death. I am not trying to make a point.' he repeated, struggling to control his voice. 'I am just trying to understand what is going on around me. Let's walk.' He picked up his bicycle and the pair walked in silence around the lake before taking a small path that led to a narrow road circling the park. Sludge lived on this road, on the opposite side of the park in one of the large Victorian houses built for local merchants and their families, but which now housed divers departments of the Social Services, a private school and an independent church, in addition to those that had been converted for multi occupancy.

The trees from the park reached across the road to meet the trees that remained in the front gardens opposite, forming a leafy arch over the road. Ann placed her hand on the bicycle saddle halting their progress and pointed at the canopy of branches overhead. 'It's so quiet and peaceful here.' she said. She moved her hand from the saddle onto Sludge's arm, 'I'm not another Jeremy Barbour, Dr Sludge.' she said. 'I'll tell you what I know and I'll tell you what I think. You can then decide what to do, if you have to do anything.' she smiled, 'OK?'

Sludge looked at the young woman and thought about inviting her to his flat, but decided against that, 'OK,' he said, 'shall we carry on walking?'

They walked slowly under the trees; the early evening sun now low in the sky behind them sending their shadows long and thin in front of them. 'If evidence is found,' Ann said, 'proving that the rumours are true, that a member of the Royal Family behaved in what could be termed a lewd and licentious manner then steps can be taken to ensure either that the story is buried and never sees the light of day, or the story together with the evidence, is given to the press, thereby discrediting that particular family member. Those are the only reasons for pursuing an issue with such vigour, either to kill it, or, for whatever reason, to publicise it. Thankfully that decision is not mine, my job is to do what it takes to find the evidence.'

'That's what you know,' said Sludge, 'but what do you think?'

Ann stopped, stared at Sludge and laughed. 'What do I think? I think I am in a dirty business where there is no black or white, only many different shades of grey. If evidence is found I have the strong feeling that it will be used to establish that one particular member of the Royal Family was a darker shade of grey than the others, and is therefore a more suitable focus for the great British public's dislike than its adoration. The rumours that have been in circulation for years will be substantiated, the press will have a field day, and a reputation will be in tatters. Do I care?' she said, kicking at a pile of leaves, 'Not really, they all piss in the same pot.' She moved to the front of the bicycle and gripped the handlebars, the front wheel between her legs as she looked directly at Sludge. 'As Barbour apparently said, if you saw it, you will know.' she said, 'Have you got it Dr Sludge? Have you got what I am looking for?'

Sludge stared down at the ground between Ann's feet. He knew that she had engaged with his vulnerability and he wanted to tell her about the package, wanted to hand it over, to be rid of it. But then he saw the image of Ronan Coyne's twisted body, and Doc Holliday's warning rang in his head, 'Beware the girl in yellow'.

'If Albert had kept anything,' he said, lifting his head and looking Ann straight in the eye, 'it will be in his house. The Society is taking an inventory on Wednesday, the day after tomorrow. I suggest that you attend. You will be welcome to take anything that you think could represent a threat to national security.'

Ann held his gaze, a faint smile in her eyes.

'I guess that you know the address.' said Sludge, 'Joan Sanderson and others will be there at nine o'clock. I'll telephone her and tell her to expect you, and I will also mention our agreement.'

'You won't be there?' Ann said.

'No, I'll be out of town, on University business.' Sludge said. Uncomfortable under her steady gaze he looked beyond her and saw Danny Graziano walking towards them. 'Is this guy looking for you by any chance?' he said, nodding in the direction of the approaching young man.

Ann turned and waved, 'Ah, yes, Danny. I met him this morning. He promised to show me the delights of the student bar. I said that I would meet him at your house, I hope you don't mind?'

'Hell, no,' he laughed, 'it'll do my reputation the power of good. I'll be in the University on Thursday. Why don't you meet me in the refectory around two o'clock, you can tell me about the inventory.'

'I'll do that,' she said, starting to cross the road towards Danny Graziano, who was standing a short distance away. She turned to look at Sludge as he began to ride off, 'and you'll be able to tell me about your trip to London.' she called, a rueful smile on her face as she walked towards the waiting Danny.

TWELVE

Surprise! Surprise!

As soon as possible after leaving the surprisingly large town, the train swerved to run alongside the wide slow moving umber waters of the river, hugging the northern bank for a few miles before darting across to Doncaster, then heading south through the Lincolnshire flatlands, a brief view of the Cathedral at Peterborough, and then the London villages making their promises of capital living before arriving at the reality of King's Cross.

Sludge would have taken the train, even if his car had been available to him, but he would have driven to the station, and so avoided the unseemly rush that saw him arrive at the last minute and get on board with no time to spare. Flustered, both by the fact that his taxi had been late, and that he had slept badly, Sludge thankfully settled into his seat, happy to be facing the engine. He dropped his bag and hat on the vacant adjoining seat, his book on the table, and smiled briefly at the couple sitting opposite him, a young girl, aged six or seven years he guessed, and an older man with white hair and troubled eyes, possibly her grandfather. The little girl stared at him with a candid, unselfconscious curiosity; the older man, who was indeed her grandfather, noticed her stare and attempted to distract her by pointing out of the window. Impatiently, the child shook her head and, kneeling on her seat, whispered in the grandfather's ear, one hand cupped over her mouth, the other pointing furtively at Sludge. With a shake of his head, the grandfather gently persuaded the child to sit down and bent across to talk softly to her.

Sludge opened his book and began flipping through. He had chosen *Tono Bungay*, a novel he sometimes used to contradict the argument (from marketing undergraduate students) that marketing was a late twentieth century innovation; not for that reason, but because he knew that the novel contained a particularly vivid description of the effect the coming of the railways had on the general populace. As he remembered it the advent of the steam engine into London was likened to a giant serpent crashing down across the metropolis, destroying everything in its path, its huge head devastating a space that was to become the railway station at King's Cross. He wanted to find that particular couple of paragraphs so that he could read them in detail, he wasn't sure why. While he skimmed the pages he was aware of the comfortable drone from his travelling companions, the girl's sharp enquiring tones matched with the warm tenderness of the grandfather's voice in which resonated the evidence of unconditional love.

'Is that the seaside, Grandpa?' said the little girl excitedly, pointing out of the train window at the river bank, no more than twenty meters away.

'Seaside?' chuckled the grandfather, gently moving the girl back so that her nose wasn't so close to the window, 'No, love, that's not the seaside. That is the widest river in England.'

'It looks like seaside.' said the girl doubtfully, looking at the strip of shingle lapped by the river.

'Yes, it does,' agreed the grandfather, 'do you remember crossing that very big bridge when your daddy brought you to stay with me, while he got your new house ready?' he said, watching the reflection of his granddaughter's face in the window. She nodded, her expression relaxed, but serious. 'Well, very soon we will be going under that bridge, it's the biggest bridge in the world.'

'Yes,' the little girl sighed, 'even if it isn't the seaside it still looks nicer than Shrivellsea'.

'Do you really think so?' said the grandfather, smiling at Sludge, who, at the mention of Shrivellsea, had looked up from his book. 'We went there for the day,' the older man explained to Sludge, 'Emily here,' he nodded to his granddaughter who had moved to look at Sludge, 'didn't think much of it at all.'

'In my book that makes you an excellent judge.' said Sludge, meeting the girl's unwavering gaze. Emily continued to stare at Sludge although she turned her head towards her grandfather.

'You can ask him now,' she said, 'because he's talking to us.'

Sludge transferred his gaze from the girl to her grandfather and raised his eyebrows. 'You want to ask me something?' he said.

'Ah,' said the man looking quickly from Sludge to Emily and back again, 'it's a little embarrassing,' he hesitated.

'Go on, grandpa,' insisted the girl, 'ask him. He said you can.'

Sludge sat back in his seat enjoying the moment created by the older man's good humoured discomfiture, and the girl's clear focus. She hadn't yet moved from the straightforward uncomplicated nature of childhood; time enough, thought Sludge smiling.

'Emily would like to know,' said the grandfather, the sadness in his eyes partially offset by the light of laughter, 'it's your hat you see. Emily would like to know. Are you a cowboy?'

A low chuckle accompanied his broad grin as Sludge shook his head and said 'No, I'm not a cowboy,' but on seeing the crestfallen look on the face of the little girl, he quickly added, 'although the hat does belong to a cowboy, a friend of mine. He lives in America, in a small town called Durango, high in the Rocky Mountains and sometimes comes to England. I've heard that he is in London, so I am going to find him and return his hat.'

Wide eyed, the girl looked from Sludge to her grandfather and back to Sludge, 'What do they call him?' she said.

Sludge leaned across the table. 'They call him,' he said dropping his voice to a confidential whisper, 'the Durango Kid, and he rides a pure white horse called Blaze. He rides around this big place called Colorado looking for people who need help; when he finds them, he helps them. He's coming to London for a little holiday.'

'I used to have a pony,' said Emily, 'but he's staying with Mummy now. Daddy says that I can still go to see him.' The little girl regarded Sludge pensively. 'Is your friend bringing his horse with him?'

Sludge felt a sudden stab of pain at the picture painted by Emily's words. He looked quickly across at the grandfather who was staring down at his granddaughter.

'No,' said Sludge, 'he isn't bringing his horse. Blaze has gone to stay with some other horses. He's having a holiday as well.'

Satisfied with the answer Emily smiled at Sludge as he sat back in his seat. Her grandfather removed his glasses and wiped his eyes. Sludge, who was only too aware of his own fragility and didn't want to develop the story or become further involved, glanced out of the window. 'Look,' he said pointing, 'here is the bridge.' The little girl twisted in her seat to look in the direction Sludge was pointing and her grandfather leaned across her to catch sight of the bridge, probably not the biggest in the world, but a magnificent sight for all that as the single span arched majestically between towers more than a mile apart.

Making a round trip, that is, crossing the bridge and back after starting at the north bank car park was just less than four miles. This made it a popular venue for charity walks. Most weekends the bridge was crowded with a great variety of people supporting any number of worthy causes, so crowded in fact that runners, joggers and serious walkers kept away. Today being Wednesday the pedestrian pathway was deserted apart from two runners, a man and a woman running side by side.

Although the distance was too great for Sludge to see their faces, he nevertheless recognised the couple as they often ran through the park near his flat. The goatee-bearded man had a nut brown bald head and the woman had long, silver blonde hair fastened back in a ponytail that swung from side to side as she ran. He didn't know either of them, but had seen them so often running through different areas, that unconsciously they had become part of his life. Once he saw them taking their ease in a small coffee bar on Oldlands Avenue, near the University; given the opportunity to consider them closely, he was quite shocked to realise that the couple, fit looking and stylish, were both beyond late middle age. When they got up to leave the man put on a large black hat and grinned at Sludge, as if to acknowledge membership of the 'big hat club'. Sludge had touched the brim of his hat and returned the grin. Observing them in the café, he had realised that the two were completely together, utterly at ease with each other, the sort of people who were never truly apart. As the train took him under the bridge and them from his sight he muttered, 'Was it in another lifetime?'

'Excuse me?' the grandfather said. Sludge looked at him uncomprehendingly.

'You spoke,' he explained, 'something about lifetime, I think.'

'Sorry,' said Sludge 'I was just thinking aloud.'

Emily tugged at her grandfather's sleeve, 'Can we get a drink now, please, granddad?' she said.

'Yes we can,' he replied standing up, 'the buffet car is this way.' He took the girl's hand, 'Can we bring you anything?' he said, looking at Sludge.

'That's kind of you, but no thanks.' Sludge said, patting the bag at his side. There was nothing in the bag, but he didn't want to prolong contact with the couple in case he involuntarily learned more about the sadness in their lives, and he was very tired. When Emily and her grandfather returned carrying drinks, crisps and chocolate, Sludge was asleep.

'You must have a clear conscience, you slept like a baby'. The grandfather smiled at Sludge, having shaken him into wakefulness as the train pulled into King's Cross.

'If only that was true,' Sludge smiled at the man standing alongside, 'I didn't sleep much last night.' He yawned and rubbed his face vigorously before picking up his hat.

The little girl was watching him carefully. 'I hope that you find your friend.' she said. 'If you do will you buy another hat for your self?'

His brain still partly fogged by sleep, he was momentarily puzzled by the girl's remark.

'The Durango Kid.' prompted the older man.

'Ah, yes,' said Sludge, 'thank you, I am sure that I will find him. And then I will buy another hat, like this, but with a silver band around it.'

Emily smiled at him, and then at her grandfather as he took her hand, led her down the carriage and out onto the platform. They both waved to Sludge as they caught sight of him through the window. A few minutes later, he was standing on the main concourse of the station. He looked at his watch; it was just after eleven o'clock. As his appointment was at twelve thirty, and because he detested travelling by the underground, he decided to walk to the City Wall to find the offices of Cuthbert, Dibble and

Grubb. He estimated that would take him rather less than an hour.

He walked up the Euston Road as far as Tolmer's Square, for no reason other than his favourite African author, Dambudzo Marechera squatted there in the 1970s while he was writing *Black Sunlight* and *The Black Insider*. Cutting across the road to Malet Street on his way to the City, he passed by University College where he had been called for his *viva voce*. Just for a moment, he stopped outside the impressive doors of the College English Department, but realising that it meant nothing to him, he walked on. Although he was reasonably familiar with London and didn't really expect to find Cuthbert, Dibble and Grubb housed in Dickensian conditions, he was nevertheless disappointed to find that the address he had been given on City Wall was a modern multi storey office block. '1950s modern,' he muttered to himself as he squinted up at the uneasy mixture of concrete, glass and mosaic tiling, 'more Becket than Dickens'. He took the lift up to the twelfth floor, turned left as indicated, walked about fifteen yards and found the solicitor's offices on his right. The door was half glazed with, written in black letters on the grey opaque glass, the names 'Cuthbert, Dibble and Grubb' were arranged in a half-moon above the word, 'Solicitors' and beneath that the invitation to, 'Please walk in'.

He entered a small room that although windowless, was surprisingly airy. The walls were painted a fresh pale green and plain, apart from a watercolour of a red sailed fishing boat crossing an estuary. On one side of the room stood a small deep maroon two seater settee and two matching chairs around a low table carrying a neat pile of magazines; on the other side, a mahogany desk holding a computer screen and keyboard and a framed photograph of a family group. Pushed back from the desk was an empty chair. Directly opposite him was a door, just as he was wondering whether to knock on it, the door opened and a friendly-faced, elderly-looking woman emerged carrying a bundle of papers.

'Hello,' she said brightly, 'you must be Dr Ludgeworth.' Sludge nodded. 'Please take a seat, I'll tell Mr Cuthbert that you are here.' She pointed at the settee and went back through the door, re-emerging no more than a minute later. 'Please come this way.' she said. He followed her and was surprised to find that the door opened directly on to a staircase. Facing him at the top of the stairs was a short corridor painted the same shade of green as the downstairs room, a small window at the end through which he could see only sky. He noticed identical heavy oak doors, two on either side of the corridor. The woman led him to the one that was standing ajar, knocked, pushed the door open and after saying, 'Dr Ludgeworth, Mr Cuthbert.' stepped back so that Sludge could enter the room.

Charles Cuthbert, a tall man with an avuncular air, an immaculate pin striped suit and well-groomed hair swept back either side of an arrow-straight side parting, stood up from his desk and held out his hand. 'Dr Ludgeworth,' he said, his voice rich and deep, 'it's good to meet you. I trust you had a pleasant journey down.'

Sludge took the outstretched hand, suppressed a smile at the Masonic implications of the grip, and said, 'Mr Cuthbert, thank you, yes.'

Pointing to a worn dark green leather chair on the other side of his very large desk the solicitor invited Sludge to sit down. 'Have you seen a partner's desk before?' he asked.

'No, I haven't.' said Sludge looking at the desk.

'This is a particularly fine example. My great-great grandfather Josiah Cuthbert acquired it, when, together with his partner, Septimus Dibble, he founded the firm in 1825.' He ran his hands gently across the surface of the desk, 'I like to think of them, first in a small room in York Buildings, and then later on in bigger premises on Grey's Inn Road, beavering away across this desk When the firm moved here in the Sixties my father transferred as much of the furniture as he could accommodate.'

Sludge smiled and looked around the room. It was comfortably furnished, a bookcase, a tall double-doored cabinet, both in the same very good oak of the desk and three four drawer filing cabinets, also in wood, but much later than the desk. On the pale cream walls were several old photographs; among them he was surprised to see the rather gloomy moustached face of Thomas Hardy.

'Is that Thomas Hardy?' he asked.

'Ah, yes,' Mr Cuthbert confirmed, 'he was a valued client. We have tended to specialise in the literary world. You know, of course that the late Albert Bleaney engineered this meeting?' The solicitor accepted Sludge's nod and continued, 'Apparently, Mr Bleaney came across a reference to us in a work about Hardy. We, how shall I say, attended to the more unusual aspects of Hardy's affairs, and that led Mr Bleaney to our door, as he was proposing something not quite straightforward.' He said this while staring at Thomas Hardy's image, but now turned back to face Sludge, 'Can I see your passport, please'.

'Of course.' Sludge said. Reaching into his bag he rummaged briefly before locating the passport, which he placed on the desk.

Mr Cuthbert picked it up and examined it carefully before he was satisfied. He then reached into the top right hand drawer and took out an envelope from which he extracted a sheet of paper. 'Mr Bleaney was concerned to make certain that the material he left should only be placed in the hands of Dr William Ludgeworth.' he said, 'To that end, apart from insisting on physical confirmation of identity, he left a series of questions. I understand that only Dr Ludgeworth can answer them.'

'What happens if I get one wrong?' said Sludge with an air of concern and doubt.

'Quite simply our business will finish at that point and the material will be destroyed unopened.' said the solicitor softly, but with great authority. He took a photograph from the envelope and passed it to Sludge. 'I want you to tell me three things,' he consulted his sheet of paper, 'firstly, name all the people in the photograph, then tell me where it took place, and finally, what was the occasion'.

Sludge considered the photograph. It showed himself, Albert Bleaney and Harry Cooper, sitting on a wooden bench in a garden he recognised as belonging to 105 West Bank. He had never seen the photograph before. 'I am on the left,' he said, 'Albert Bleaney is next to me, and on the right is Harry Cooper, landlord of The Brickmakers. The photograph was taken in Albert's garden at 105 West Bank.' He looked up briefly, and then returned to study the photograph. The three men were obviously in good spirits, smiling at the camera, holding up glasses as if in a toast. Looking more closely, he saw that he was holding a small oblong box in his left hand. Puzzled, he looked up at the solicitor who was watching him with interest. In complete silence he gazed at the photograph for several minutes. Then he remembered.

Sludge placed the photograph on the desk, stood up and walked to the window. 'Harry Cooper was a crossword fanatic.' He said looking across the London skyscape to the river, over to his left he could see the London Eye turning slowly. 'We, that is Albert and me, sometimes helped him out with the prize crossword, in the Independent I think. Whatever the paper was, the prize he was trying to win was a Montblanc fountain pen. To cut a long story short, after years of trying he was successful; he did actually win such a pen. I was with Albert at his home when Harry telephoned to tell him that the pen had arrived; when he heard that I was there he insisted on coming round for a celebration.'

Sludge moved away from the window and returned to sit opposite Mr Cuthbert. 'As I remember it, that photograph was taken by Molly, who was living with Albert at the time, and it shows the three of us celebrating success in a crossword competition.' He picked up the photograph and stared at it again before looking up. 'I've never seen this before, it would have been taken about a year before Albert died.'

Charles Cuthbert consulted the paper on his desk, 'I don't have a date,' he said, 'as for the photograph, if all goes well, I can see no reason why you shouldn't keep it.' He looked at the paper again, 'What happened to the pen?' he said.

'Harry insisted that as it had been a joint effort, he hadn't got an automatic right to keep the prize. We wanted him to keep it, but he was adamant that we should all have a chance. After some debate we agreed to draw lots to decide who should keep the pen.'

Sludge reached inside his jacket and took out a tortoiseshell Montblanc fountain pen. 'I won.' he said, placing the pen on the desk in front of the smiling solicitor.

'No more questions Dr Ludgeworth. I am satisfied that you are who you say you are. And I can happily fulfil my duties by handing over to you the material left with us by the late Albert Bleaney. To be perfectly honest I recognised you as soon as you walked in. I remember that Mr Bleaney spoke of you with great warmth and described you as a man of distinctive style. Please excuse me,' he said as he picked up the telephone and pressed two numbers, 'Mabel,' he said after a short pause, 'please bring the Bleaney file to my room.' He replaced the telephone. 'Do you want to take a first look at the material while you're here?' he said, 'There is a suitable room directly opposite mine.'

Sludge was surprised to find that his throat had suddenly become very dry and he had to swallow hard before he could speak. 'Yes please,' he croaked, 'that seems a good idea.'

'I'll have Mrs McGregor bring you a coffee.' he said, standing up and walking to the door. 'I'll show you the room.'

Standing just inside the entrance of the other room as Mr Cuthbert talked to Mrs McGregor in the corridor outside, Sludge looked around him. To his right, a high window with vertical blinds, in front of him a mahogany table with an inlaid leather top on which stood an ancient inkwell holder. Four chairs were arranged asymmetrically at the table with three on one side. To his left, a small coffee table was flanked by two very old and worn leather armchairs.

'Sorry about that.' said Mr Cuthbert as he entered the room carrying a box file. 'Here we are.' he said as he opened the box and took out two envelopes and a package and placed them on the larger table, the envelopes on top of the package. 'Here is the document signed by Mr Albert Bleaney in which he asked us to keep a sealed package and two sealed envelopes - please read it.' He handed a single sheet of paper to Sludge.

'Yes, that is what it says.' Sludge acknowledged.

'Good, please sign here,' he placed another sheet of paper on the desk, 'you are simply signing to confirm that two sealed envelopes and a sealed package, formerly the property of Mr Albert Bleaney, have been placed in your possession.' He smiled as Sludge signed the paper. 'How very appropriate that you are using that pen. Mabel will bring your coffee shortly. If you need anything you can call her on double eight, ' he pointed to the telephone, 'or, just rap on my door.'

Standing at the table, Sludge nodded, 'Thanks.' he said as the solicitor left the room.

The cold-eyed man stared down at the envelopes and the package. One of the envelopes had writing on. He recognised Albert Bleaney's neat hand. The message read, 'Open the other one first.' He picked up the envelope and saw a message written on the second envelope, it read, 'Open this one first.'

THIRTEEN

Open This One First

Sludge sat down at the table and looked at the package. It was A4 size, wrapped in plain brown paper and bound with string. Red sealing wax had been dripped across the knots. He picked it up and inspected all sides; its weight suggested it held three or four fairly substantial notebooks. He noticed nothing was written on the wrapping.

The envelopes, also sealed with blobs of red wax, he placed side-by-side. Lost in thought, he looked at them for several minutes before he selected the one that advised it should be opened first. Using a bone handled letter opener from the desk, he carefully slit the envelope open. The good quality paper crackled as he took out the letter out and unfolded it. Realising that he had been holding his breath for some time, he exhaled noisily as he unfolded the two-pages. He stared at the writing, seeing nothing, until his eyes focussed, and he began to read.

Dear Billy
(he read)
Apparently I have only a few weeks to live (how's that for an opening!) - most of my affairs will be taken care of by my will, but there are a couple of things I have decided I want to leave to you to resolve. I cannot say how long after my death you will receive this letter, indeed whether you will receive it all.

I am still not certain that I am doing the right thing - and so your discovery of this letter and what goes with it has been left partly to chance. As I couldn't make my mind up, I have left myself the option that you may not receive *this letter at all, if that is the case, what I am about to reveal will <u>never</u> be revealed. Confused? You will be, read on!*

Charles Cuthbert (or his successor) - will have given you two sealed envelopes and a sealed package. If you have followed my instructions, you are reading this letter first. The other letter contains an extract from my diary - yes, I did keep a diary, but it was not something I was very disciplined about. As I am not asking you to be my Boswell, I destroyed the diary, apart from one entry. That piece recounts a most remarkable experience, one I believe that led to the interest of those determined young men from national security. The artefact mentioned there is not included here. Thomas Hardy will be able to help you - again, I have left something to chance. I could say more than that but I don't feel the need to add to the words I recorded some years ago, directly after the event.

The other package contains my workbooks. I never mentioned them to anyone, because, well I don't know why, I suppose when I had put about the idea that I destroyed my notes as soon as I was happy with a poem, it would have seemed foolish to announce that I hadn't done that at all. Overall, the tactic worked in that it kept me blessedly free of the professional 'lit crit' types. (No offence, Billy, I've never seen you like that.)

You will find the workbooks are a complete record of my work. It was my habit to work on one poem at a time, taking it through several drafts before settling on a final version. You will also find that there is quite a lot of unpublished material. For my benefit I used a simple colour coded system for classifying the poems -I am sure that you will work it out.

I hesitate to use the word legacy, Billy, but I suppose that this letter, the diary extract, and my workbooks are just that. I give them to you free of encumbrance and without let or hindrance (thank Charles Cuthbert for that last bit!), to do with as you see fit. I imagine that the workbooks will present you with a publishing opportunity - if that is what you choose.

As for the diary extract and the 'artefact' (should you find it) - it is possible that the Security boys would eventually have needled me to the extent that I would have betrayed a secret. What you do depends on a great many things, not least of which I suppose is whether you still feel that you have no obligation to give 'loyalty to royalty'. Do you remember saying that, I wonder.

I realise that this 'legacy' presents you with problems Billy, as you may have to shake off the comfort blanket of existence at the University and interrupt the quiet flow of your life. Perhaps that is my intention - again, I am not sure I should risk that, so that's another reason for hedging my bets that you may never get this far.

I remember trying to convince you that Bob Dylan had a phrase for every occasion (we must have been drunk!), well - I have just spent a fruitless hour or so searching for something apposite to this situation and I haven't found anything suitable. So, all I can say is - you were a good friend Billy, thanks for that.

Albert
December 2nd 1996

Sludge laid the letter on the table and stared into space, overwhelmed by the sense that Albert Bleaney was in the room. A deep sigh caught in his throat and brought with it an involuntary sob that caught him unawares. Distracted he brushed unexpected tears from his cheeks and stared at the letter.

There was, he was quite aware, far too much information to absorb at one reading. In any event, he realised that he was not in the right frame of mind to start taking notes, better to read through all the material first. He glanced at the package, then at the other envelope, before picking up the opened letter, which he read again before putting it to one side.

'Open the other one first,' he muttered to himself, 'it doesn't say, 'and then open me next', so...', he pulled the package forward and began picking at the sealing wax. Memories of Christmas past flooded over him as he felt the string in his fingers and smelt the brown paper, heard the thin crackle as it tore. He unpacked five A4 size notebooks, each one was black with a red spine, and laid them out on the desk. The notebooks were identical, except for being numbered one to five. His realised his hand was shaking as he picked up number one, opened it, and stared at the first page.

After sitting motionless for several minutes, Sludge closed the book and walked across to the small table on which, as a precaution against accidents, Mrs MacGregor had placed a pot of coffee and a plate of biscuits. He drank some coffee while standing, replaced his cup on the table and sat down again at the desk. With a deep sigh, he re-opened notebook one, and began flicking through the pages.

The first entry in the notebook was an exact copy of *The Best Days of Your Life*, which Sludge recognised as the first poem Albert had published, when he was about nineteen or twenty years old. Subsequent poems were - as the letter suggested - taken through several drafts before a final version, neatly written out with the title underlined in either red or green; Albert's simple colour coded system. Sludge soon realised that the 'red' poems were those intended for publication because he recognised them, the 'green' poems were unpublished and completely new to him, and to anyone else he was certain. Working quickly, he looked through each of the five workbooks in turn, recording the title of each 'green' poem after reading the finished version just once. At least that was the intention, but he found some so captivating that he read them again immediately. After a couple of hours or so, he had a list of one hundred and thirty-five unpublished poems.

The new poems were an absolute revelation. Whereas Albert's published output chiefly engaged with the world of work in realistic fashion, and very often with the inequalities encouraged (he argued) by the inherent contradictions within the capitalist system, the unpublished work was drawn from the completely different arena of his personal life.

Here were scenes from his youth such as *On Corpo Field*, *Lord Corpulent's Complaint* and *Johnnie Steen's Century*, tender poems, wistful, at times achingly funny. Here were scenes from later life, such as the idyllic *View from Top Path* and his distress at the developments in his birthplace *Ottingham, Oh, My Ottingham*. The beautiful, though almost unbearably moving lament on the distress he had seen in Sludge following the death of his father, called simply, *Ode to Billy Sludge*.

However, most staggering of all were the love poems. Sludge estimated that more than a third of the new material concerned Albert's individual relationships with Molly, Joan, Beryl and June. Here in the love poems Albert revealed himself as a lyric poet of the finest quality. Here was the incisive self-awareness of *Bleaney's Blues* detailing the despair of his being unable to commit to one woman. Here was the haunting vision of ephemeral memories in *Shadows*: the sheer beauty of *Image in the Rain* and *Dreaming of Rainbows*; the gentle and delicate *Molly, Molly, Molly*; the unadulterated joy and energy of *Beryl's Return*; and the surprise of the salacious celebrations of *A Promising Position*.

Sludge leaned back in his chair and gazed at the list of poems. He was stunned. Albert Bleaney had a well-deserved reputation as a fine poet, but the new work showed he had a much more extensive range than that revealed by the published work. Known as a capable wordsmith and as a reliable craftsman, the notebooks showed him to be so much more than that. Even at this early stage Sludge knew that he would have the poems published. An act that would bring about the re-evaluation of the poet and, Sludge was convinced, elevate him to the status of one of the foremost poets of the twentieth century. Additionally, already referred to as the 'famous four', publication would, he realised, greatly increase the fame of 'Albert's women'. Whether that would be welcomed or not, only time would tell.

'This is the stuff of genius, Albert old son,' he murmured, staring at the list and drifting into a reverie, 'but why did you keep it such a secret?' The events of recent days had taken a toll on Sludge mentally and he knew that he was in not in the right state of mind to begin a thorough examination of the notebooks. Even at first glimpse, the realisation of an unknown and unsuspected aspect of his close friend was quite overwhelming. Sludge realised with a detached dismay that the darkness around the edges of his mind was closing in as he struggled to keep control of his emotions. In spite of the encroaching mist, he was convinced that publication of the new poems could have an even bigger impact than the (also posthumous) publication of Ted Hughes *Birthday Letters*. He also knew that he had to read the contents of the other envelope before he left the solicitor's office.

With a preoccupied air, Sludge folded Albert's letter and replaced it in the envelope. The list of new poems he placed inside the first page of notebook one. He then stacked the notebooks in numerical order and placed them neatly on the left hand side of the desk. After a moments thought he placed the opened envelope on top of the pile and then picked up the unopened envelope, weighing it in his hands as he did so.

Shaking his head impatiently a couple of times, as if to clear something from his mind, Sludge slit open the envelope and extracted several triple folded pages, obviously torn out of a notebook. He smoothed the pages flat, and began to read.

17th July 1985
If I had kept a regular diary then this page would have followed on like any other, but as I haven't, I notice that the previous entry was in January, six and a half months ago, recording the momentous arrival of a late Christmas card! I suppose one of the reasons that I have never kept a regular diary is that I tend to ramble on - although that may well be one of the attractions - the recording of the detritus of daily living that somehow, after a suitable period of time, assumes historical and sociological significance. Perhaps not - I think it was Thomas Carlyle

who said 'A well-written life is almost as rare as a well-spent one.' - rarer, I would have said. However, I digress.

I have dated this entry as above, but in truth, it is already the next day. I am sitting at my desk looking out on a silent and deserted street (little wonder, it is two-thirty in the morning!). I think I saw an owl glide through the halo of the street light across from my house just now, but I can't be sure - more of an impression than a sighting.

Yesterday (the 17th) was a most remarkable day. I went to Buckingham Palace to be invested by HM the Queen with the Order of the British Empire (Empire? What Empire?). A remarkable event in itself, but what happened immediately after the investiture surpassed even that experience.

The day did not start well. Joan had agreed to come with me although she argued that by accepting the award I was compromising my republican principles (such as they are - I fear that she sometimes mistakes rhetoric for passion). At the last minute, she changed her mind and I went to Buckingham Palace alone. (Were I an authentic diarist my 'republican principles' and my relationship with Joan would have been explored in depth already, but as I am not - and that's a matter of design and choice - they haven't!!)

I may write about the investiture itself at sometime, but probably not, as it was little more than an exercise in queuing and waiting around in opulent surroundings and being herded from here to there by self important minions; until finally, I stood in front of my monarch to receive my medal and sixty seconds of glory. And then it was straight into the garden (grounds I suppose I should say) and thankfully, the alcohol.

Small groups were dotted about the lawns, drinking champagne and looking out for the really famous. I was talking to a surprisingly tall jockey and a jolly red faced social worker from Bristol (both pretended to be familiar with my work) when a short swarthy character approached us and addressed me by name. He asked me to follow him as 'a very special person' wanted to meet me. Intrigued by the man's sullen demeanour and encouraged by my natural curiosity I went along with him.

We went back into the palace and, as far as I could tell, walked straight across to emerge into a more informal garden area. Still ignoring my attempts at conversation except for the occasional 'si' or (strangely) 'niet', he led me to a small copse.

'In there.' he said, indicating a narrow path. The path took me to a small clearing, completely hidden by the surrounding trees. At the far end of the clearing, no more than four or five metres away, was a wooden bench. To my great astonishment, sitting on the bench, head bent over a book she was holding, was one of the most photographed women in the world, the 'bloom of Britain' herself. She looked up and giggled, as a voice called out from somewhere behind me and to my left, 'He's here, precious one.'

As she walked towards me I was surprised to note that she was very tall, only an inch or so short of six feet I guess; she was also on the heavy side of slim, although the grace of her movement brought the words 'slender' and 'lithe' to mind. I retain a sense of her elegance, although her clothes were very simple; a short straight black skirt and a long sleeved loose fitting deep maroon silk shirt open at the neck. The famous golden hair was tied loosely at the nape of her neck and her head held erect in what had become her stereotypical image, the bold Princess looking the world directly in the face. As I took her outstretched hand (not knowing whether to bow or not I settled for a brisk nod) and at once sensed a palpable, untamed (untameable?) air of sexuality.

Holding my hand in a firm but light grip that I have to admit was sending waves straight to my groin, she said, 'Hello, Mr Bleaney, can I call you Albert?' I think I nodded or mumbled some sort of consent, (I really was stupidly overwhelmed) because she said with another giggle 'You can call me Princess,' she then raised her voice and looking in the direction of the voice from the trees added, 'everyone calls me Princess, except for a very naughty boy called Lombardo'. Apparently, Lombardo was the surly individual who had brought me to meet her. When I asked (I was at a loss for anything intelligent to say) if he was Italian she roared with laughter and said, again in a loud voice, 'Italian? He'd like to think so, but there is more Birmingham than Bologna in our darling Bardo.'

The Princess linked her arm in mine and we walked to the bench, which I noticed was covered with petals or blossom. Her scent, pheromonal rather than cosmetic, was overpowering me, and I was glad to sit down. She sat down no more than a body width away and passed me the book she had been reading; it was a copy of my first collection, I Saw My Brother Marching*. Apparently, she had always liked my work because, as she explained, they were like fairy stories (!), because they described a world of which she knew nothing. I read some poems to her at her request and she listened attentively, asking questions, but questions about me rather than the poems, mainly* *about the feelings and emotions I experienced when writing or reading. I didn't get the sense of a great intellect at work, but there was a quest for meaning, for understanding, which on reflection I fear may be beyond her. Due perhaps to inadequate (over-indulgent?) schooling, or I suppose that she may not be very bright. However she did show the ability to inspire confidences, when she asked me about the title poem I told her the truth about how it came about - a story I haven't told anyone else. When I think of it now I can hardly believe that I did that - the woman held me in thrall by her presence, that is the only explanation. I think I would have told her anything.*

We talked about the poems, she told me a little about her life (not very happy), and asked questions about mine. I do not know how long I had been there, half an hour perhaps, when Lombardo called from the trees in a sing song voice, 'Time to go home. Time to go home.' a short pause then, 'Albert is waving bye-bye, bye-bye.'

I felt at the time that the Princess's rage was staged and part of a pattern of behaviour designed to sustain the apparently odd relationship between her and Lombardo. Whatever the reason, she jumped to her feet and screamed, 'Bardo, you're a very naughty boy. Come out of there at once and apologise to Mr Bleaney.' She had walked forward a couple of paces or so and as she was standing almost directly in front me I couldn't help noticing that several petals had stuck to the seat of her skirt. She glanced over her shoulder; gave me that famous 'look from beneath lowered lashes' and said, 'Why Albert, I do believe that you are looking at my bottom.' Of course, I was, but flustered, I stuttered an explanation about the petals. In response, she asked me to remove them and told me to pick them one at a time.

So that I could do this, she kept her back to me, and bent forward slightly with her hands on her knees. I thought at the time that I was being presented with a sight to beat all others - but something more was to follow, and soon.

It is small wonder that thoughts of Lombardo had been driven from my mind, and I was taken aback when he suddenly appeared, very red faced, and demanded an explanation from me. Before I could reply the Princess intervened and a shrill exchange of views commenced including such gems as, from the Princess, 'Daddy says you're as queer as a five shilling note', which received the rejoinder from Lombardo, 'The ugly little man only said that because I refused to touch his dick'. Once more, I was struck by the theatrical behaviour of both and have since wondered how and why they came to define their respective roles in this way. The argument, which had flared with an abrupt violence, appeared to be about to blow itself out when Lombardo aimed a comment at me that proved to be a catalyst to the most extraordinary action.

He pointed at me and sneered that I was gripping the petals (plucked from the Princess's bottom) in my 'sweaty little hand' and that I was going to sneak away with them as a 'pathetic and sordid souvenir'.

The Princess, suddenly very calm, turned to me when Lombardo made his 'souvenir' remark and said 'We can find you something better than that.' still looking at me, she said, 'Give Mr Bleaney the scissors'.

I glanced at Lombardo to see he was transfixed, an uncomprehending, stupid almost, look on his face - then incomprehension became horror and to my amazement, he dropped onto his knees, saying, 'No, no, not that, not for him, precious one, not for him'. She touched the top of his head, almost in benediction, smiled at me, and repeated, 'Give him the scissors, Lombardo.' Still on his knees, Lombardo shuffled across to me, reached inside his jacket and took out a small pair of scissors that he passed over to me with obvious reluctance. I was both embarrassed and nonplussed - I stood holding the scissors, Lombardo on his knees, silent tears beginning to run down his face while the Princess gazed at us with a beatific smile.

'Lombardo,' she said' 'go and stand over there.' Sobbing quietly, but not very convincingly, the sad creature got off his knees and slowly slunk to the point indicated close by.

'Well, Albert,' said the Princess, 'you will see how badly that naughty boy treats his 'precious one'.' With no more ado, she gripped the hem of her skirt and hoisted it up to her waist. 'No, look,' she demanded, as instinctively and involuntarily, I looked away. I did look, and saw she had very long legs that were heavy in the thigh and that she was wearing white knickers (old fashioned word, I think!) with an emblem of three feathers on the front. 'Well,' she said, 'what do you think?'

I didn't know what to think or to say - I couldn't believe what I was looking at, or what I was supposed to comment on, so I mumbled something about the symbolism of the feathers.

'No, not that,' she said in an exasperated manner, 'I only wear these to annoy you-know-who.' She pushed her pelvis towards me, 'Look closer, Albert,' she commanded, 'see how Lombardo has neglected me, see how untidy I am.' I still did not know what was required of me and

stood there with the unhappy Lombardo looking on, blowing his nose in extravagant fashion.

'It will be better if you sit on the bench.' the Princess told me. I did as she ordered and she strode towards me with her skirt around her waist, coming to a stop no more than twelve inches in front of me, her legs were apart and as she was tall and I was slumped on the bench, her crotch was almost in my face. I saw then what she was talking about; she had the most luxuriant pubic hair bulging from the sides of her knickers, like straw out of a mattress.

'Lombardo is supposed to keep me tidy, but he has neglected me - as you can see.'

I was dimly aware that Lombardo replied, but I was drowning in waves of pheromones, and could hardly have reacted if he had fired a cannon. I was only aware of the Princess, her voice, her smell and the closeness of her sex. From above my head her voice drifted down, 'Take some from the middle.' she whispered, as she moved even closer to me. Completely under her spell, trembling uncontrollably and holding the scissors in my right hand, I placed my left hand between her thighs and gripped a moist tuft of hair, as I did so my knuckles brushed against her vulva, bringing a sigh and a gentle admonishment from the Princess, 'For God's sake don't do that with the scissors Albert.' she said.

To stop my hand from shaking I had to rest it against the warmth of her inner thigh as I manoeuvred the scissors into place and snipped. I remember feeling very awkward sitting there, scissors in one hand, while the other held a curl of pubic hair between finger and thumb, the petals still in my palm under the other fingers. The Princess stepped back and adjusted her skirt, she smiled as she did so and suggested that I should find something in which to place my 'souvenirs'.

At this point Lombardo intervened. He walked briskly across to me and took the scissors from my hand. He then removed the official name badge that was clipped to my jacket, took out the name card, held up the resulting empty plastic envelope and said, 'This will do.'

The Princess was delighted; she clapped her hands and cried, 'Super idea, well done, Lombardo.'

I took the envelope from him and placed the items in there. Unbelievably (I really was in a complete fog!) I then began to reattach it (now containing pubic hair and petals) to my jacket. The Princess screamed with delight at my stupidity. I think that I just grinned and sat there, having put my souvenir in my pocket, but not knowing what to do next. Her shoulders shaking with laughter she took my name badge from Lombardo and asked me if she could keep it, 'as a bookmark' - I agreed of course and, thinking I had to do something, offered to sign it. With another scream of delight, she accepted my offer and I signed the card with a Buckingham Palace biro I had picked up earlier. For a moment I thought this episode was going to take an even more bizarre turn when she took my pen and asked for the plastic envelope. I thought she was about to put her signature on the back, instead she wrote the date. 'Our secret, Albert,' she said, handing the envelope and pen back to me, 'I want you to keep it in a very safe place.'

The Princess bent forward, kissed me on the cheek, and said, 'Lombardo will show you back to the circus.' and then quickly walked behind the bench and took the path through the trees.

Lombardo led me in the opposite direction and spoke only once. Just before he pointed my way forward he stopped and, in a soft voice, in which the industrial midlands was suddenly very apparent, he asked me to return the Princess's gift. At my immediate refusal he became upset and agitated, 'The Princess has many enemies in this place,' he said, 'if they knew of her generosity things would go very badly indeed for her'.

Sludge turned the page and was surprised to find that he had come to the end. He quickly glanced through the other pages in case somehow they had become disordered. He spread them out in front of him to check that they followed on from each other. The pages were in order and he hadn't missed any out, for whatever reason that must forever remain unknown, the diary extract finished abruptly.

Sludge stared at the pages while in abstracted fashion he reached inside his jacket to locate the small plastic envelope. His fingers explored the smooth surface before he placed it on the pages in front of him. He peered at the contents, and at the barely legible date. 'Is this what Ronan died for?' he muttered in bewildered consternation, 'A princess's pubic hair.'

'Dear God Albert,' he whispered, 'I didn't know you at all.'

The cold-eyed man poured himself a cup of cold coffee and walked to the window. He was worried that the kid was sinking. Over the last couple of weeks the kid's world had gone crazy and he wasn't handling it very well.

Not very well at all. And now this. The books were OK he guessed. The kid could use them, if he could get himself together. Might be able to do the right thing. Whatever that was. But the pubic hair spelled trouble, big trouble. Trouble the kid couldn't handle. What the hell was that Albert guy thinking of?

The cold-eyed man shook a cigarette proud of the packet and lifted it to his lips. Flicking a match into flame with his thumbnail he inhaled noisily before coughing a stream of blue smoke against the window. He turned sharply as the door to his right began to open. His hand went to the gun on his hip. Was the trouble starting already?

Charles Cuthbert was surprised to see Sludge standing at the window and more than a little disconcerted to see the white face and blank eyes turned towards him with no sign of recognition whatsoever. His swift glance took in the small pile of notebooks on the desk and the neat arrangement of papers 'Are you all right, Dr Ludgeworth?' he said, genuine concern in his voice. The solicitor knew from experience that such packages as Sludge had retrieved that afternoon didn't always bring welcome news.

Still not acknowledging the solicitor's enquiry Sludge left the window, sat at the desk and leaned forward, his head in his hands. Charles Cuthbert moved from the open doorway and took a chair opposite Sludge. 'Dr Ludgeworth, ' he repeated, 'are you all right?'

For what seemed several minutes the two men sat in silence until slowly Sludge lifted his head and looked at the solicitor. 'I remember my father coming into the house one day and shouting' 'It isn't fair and it isn't right.'

when I asked him what wasn't fair and right, he said, 'a black man's left leg'. He then laughed and went out again. Funny man, my Dad.' said Sludge, his voice flat and empty. He looked down at the desk again before adding quietly, 'All right? No, I'm not all right.'

Charles Cuthbert was a shrewd man. A City solicitor with all that that entails, including a well-developed understanding of the frailties of the human condition. He was also a kindly man with a sympathetic ear for his clients and a strict policy of non-involvement. However, it was clear to him that the man facing him was in great difficulty, and so for almost certainly the first time in his life he decided to ignore the demands of professional probity and to go with his gut feeling, which told him that this man needed help and needed it now. 'I came to ask the time of your train back to Kingston,' he said, 'but, if I may so advise, you do not look in a fit state to travel. Do you have any friends in London?'

'Friends in London?' Sludge repeated. 'No, I don't have any friends in London. I don't have any friends...', his voice trailed away and he stared blankly at the papers on the desk in front of him.

Charles Cuthbert stood up and looked at Sludge, concern on his face, 'If you will excuse me,' he said, 'I have to make a phone call - I will be back in a trice.'

The cold-eyed man stared briefly at the door. Was the stranger a good guy? Who can tell, he thought to himself, who can tell. He leaned back in his chair, propped his booted feet on the desk, tilted his hat over his eyes, and waited.

It was shortly before midnight the same day that Fran Cuthbert asked her husband as he re-entered the room 'How is he?'

'I've loaned him some pyjamas and a dressing gown.' said Charles Cuthbert 'He seems quite relaxed. I've agreed to take him King's Cross for the early train. I hope he manages to get some sleep.'

Charles and Fran Cuthbert lived in a large comfortable house in Islington, within easy commuting distance of the City for him and the Homerton General Hospital for Fran, where she was a consultant psychologist. Their house, which had been in the Cuthbert family for three generations, was one of the few in the area that hadn't been converted to multi occupancy. Sludge had been accommodated in a large bedroom at the back of the house that had once been the young Charles Cuthbert's, and latterly had been occupied by the youngest of the Cuthbert children until she had left to take up a post with UNICEF, in Geneva.

'What do you think of him?' said Charles, as he settled into his chair.

'I think that he is a friendly and affable man who could be very good company, if he wasn't so obviously pre-occupied.' Fran said, 'Tell me what happened after you telephoned me.'

'There's not much to tell. I invited him to stay with us overnight; he accepted, without appearing to give it much thought. He asked me if he could make a couple of telephone calls - never owned a mobile apparently - and asked for two A4 envelopes and some sellotape. Only a few minutes later he came into my room and asked me to store the sealed envelopes for a week or so until he had made appropriate arrangements. He was insistent that the envelopes be placed in a secure safe and not just locked in my desk - he was quite forceful on that. That's about it really.' he shrugged. 'We had a drink at the Magpie on the way home. You know the rest.'

'What did you talk about?'

'I did most of the talking. He didn't say much at all.' said Charles. 'Not that he was taciturn, no, not that. I agree with you, I am sure that he could be a very interesting man, but he was too deeply distracted to become involved in small talk.'

'You have empathised with your clients before Charles, and yet this is the first time you have invited one to stay here. Why him, why Dr Ludgeworth?'

'Actually, he isn't the first.' said Charles. 'I think you were attending a conference in Edinburgh when Albert Bleaney stayed here for a couple of nights in early December 1996 - do you remember?'

'Yes, I think I do.' said his wife slowly, 'Yes, yes, I do remember that.'

'Bleaney is the key. He told me about Ludgeworth; apparently, he was thrown out of America sometime in the early Eighties and never really recovered from the experience. As I remember it, Bleaney was very attached to Ludgeworth but was concerned that he was becoming unstable, a succession of family deaths had also left their mark, the loss of an elder brother was particularly tragic. He wanted to leave him something, I don't know what, but he had doubts about whether Ludgeworth would be in a fit state to take advantage of the gift, and so he left a convoluted trail that, for Ludgeworth, led to me. I met Bleaney several times in the latter half of '96 and came to like him, when I saw Ludgeworth in such difficulties I wanted to keep an eye on him, quite simply because of the Bleaney connection.'

He stopped and looked up sharply at the ceiling at a sudden noise from somewhere above his head.

'Relax, Charles,' Fran smiled, 'he's going to the bathroom. I take it you did show him.'

'I did.' Charles replied with a grin. They both sat quietly, waiting for the footsteps that would take their guest back to his room.

Fran sipped her coffee and placed the cup on the small table in front of her. 'You know I cannot make snap judgements Charles, but I will say what I observed about Dr Ludgeworth, during the two to three hours I was in his company tonight. Although he didn't say much, what he did say was of interest, and enlightening as to his state of mind. Firstly, he was very withdrawn, that level of disengagement usually indicates trauma of some description. You said he only appeared that way after he inspected Bleaney's gift. Because of what he didn't say, and the way he didn't say it, I suspect that the trauma occurred previously and he was reminded of it by a discovery or revelation this afternoon. You understand that I am guessing, don't you?'

Charles nodded 'Yes, of course, but please go on.'

'There is little more to say other than he shows clear signs of severe anxiety, and I suspect he is managing a long standing depressive illness.'

'So Bleaney was right to be concerned about him,' Charles said, leaning forward, 'and that was back in 1996. Obviously the chap hasn't been able to progress.'

'Really Charles,' said Fran, with a brisk shake of her head, 'you can't draw that conclusion. What I can say is that if I was his doctor, or a good friend, I would be concerned for his welfare. In my view, there is nothing wrong with him that a long rest and, perhaps some treatment, couldn't put right. However, I would say that mentally he is very fragile and any increase in pressure or exacerbation of the trauma could have extremely serious consequences for his long-term good health'.

Upstairs in the large comfortable bedroom the cold-eyed man lay on the bed, his hands behind his head, staring at the ceiling. He had jammed a chair under the knob of the bedroom door and placed his gun by his side. 'Come sun up,' he murmured softly, 'we ride north.'

FOURTEEN

Signor Paolo Brindisi

Sludge glanced out of the window as the train began its long curving run into Kingston Station. The city was unique in various ways, but one attribute it shared with many others, thought Sludge, as the trackside buildings flicked by ever more slowly, was that the approach by train was undeniably scruffy and dispiriting. The train was still several minutes out of the station and yet people were already crowding around the exit, anxious perhaps to leave behind the enforced proximity of others and to lose themselves in the comfortable anonymity of the city.

Sludge was irritated by this lemming-like behaviour and busied himself checking that he was not about to leave anything behind. He looked again at the small card he had been using as a bookmark. Charles Cuthbert had given it to him earlier that morning; it was his business card on which he had written his home number and the mobile numbers for both himself and Fran. He had impressed on Sludge that he was to call, 'should you need anything, anything at all, even if you don't know what you need, but know you need something, just call one of those numbers'. He had said this with such clear and simple sincerity that Sludge had been moved to tears and was quite unable to respond. Even now, he found the evidence of such selfless generosity of spirit to be very moving.

If the people leaving the train in such haste had had more on their minds than the sole purpose of their own destinations, they might have noticed the singular figure of a tall, thin, moustached man dressed in black and wearing a wide brimmed hat with a silver band, standing in the shadows at the head of the platform. If they had taken more time in disembarking, they might have seen the man step out of the shadows to greet another man similarly dressed. Kingston was not a city renowned for the idiosyncratic style of its men, to see one such figure was unusual; to see two together was little short of remarkable. The people of Kingston, like the city itself isolated on the plain of Aulderness, are noted for their insularity, and so the meeting passed largely unobserved.

'Hello Billy,' said Doc Holliday, extending his hand, 'welcome back.' he grinned.

'Hi Doc.' said Billy, shaking the outstretched hand, embarrassed that his eyes filled with tears at the warmth of the greeting.

'Signor Brindisi is waiting for us in the lounge.' Doc Holliday pointed across the station concourse to the elegant Victorian entrance to the Royal Station Hotel, 'he managed to rearrange his schedule and is leaving this afternoon rather than this morning.' The cold-eyed man nodded absently at this information and walked in silence by the side of his compadre.

Doc Holliday was shocked by Sludge's appearance and his demeanour, he seemed somehow smaller, shrunken within himself. The disjointed telephone conversation of yesterday hinted that something was wrong, but there was a flatness about him, a deadness in his eyes and in his voice that rang warning bells. Signor Brindisi was angry that his yesterday evening meeting with Sludge had been postponed, unless Sludge was careful the next few minutes could prove very difficult indeed. He took his friends arm.

'Billy,' he said, 'before you meet Signor Brindisi, you need to know that he is a very busy man and has rearranged his schedule so that we could meet this morning.' He looked anxiously at Sludge who was staring up at the vaulted ironwork leaping underneath the roof of the station. 'Billy, listen to me,' he gripped Sludge's arm tightly, 'he is a powerful man and he wants something from you. The Brindisis' of this world are used to getting what they want. Please be very careful.'

The cold-eyed man gently moved the other's hand and looked him directly in the eye. 'To save a man's life against his will is the same as killing him.' he said 'Lead on.'

Sludge had never been in the Royal Station Hotel before. Its reputation as a place of overnight stays and one-night stands, held no attractions for him. He looked around him with interest at the many signs of devotion to royalty: the photographs of the Queen and her Duke; the former King and his Queen; and then he noticed, with barely suppressed mirth, the Prince of Wales Lounge.

'Is something amusing you, Dr Ludgeworth?' Sludge started as he realised he was being addressed by a short stocky individual wearing a dark blue suit, pale blue shirt and a narrow dark blue tie that was tied with a very small knot.

'Billy,' said Doc Holliday, anxiety showing in his voice, 'this is Signor Brindisi. I…' He stopped speaking as Brindisi signalled to him by making a small gesture with his right hand.

'Please, Dr Ludgeworth' said Brindisi, the merest hint of the Mediterranean in his accent, 'take a seat. Organise some fresh coffee John Henry.' he addressed the Doc who nodded, and went in search of service. 'Now, Dr Ludgeworth', he smiled, 'how was your trip? Profitable I hope?'

'Profitable? I suppose that depends on how you define profit.' said Sludge looking at the Doc's back as he walked away. 'My apologies for last night,' he continued turning to face the man, 'I was unavoidably detained.' The cold-eyed man glanced across at Brindisi. The smart little guy had spoken and the Doc had jumped. The kid had to be careful.

'Thank you, yes', Brindisi nodded, 'it was inconvenient, but no matter. We have our meeting now. Yes?' he said with some irritation directed at a dark haired youngish woman who had approached and was hovering at a deferential distance. She advanced quickly and spoke rapidly to Brindisi in a language Sludge recognised as Italian. He didn't speak the language although he had an intention to learn it sometime. Brindisi listened to the woman in silence then waved her away.

'Apparently we have even less time than planned.' he said to Sludge. 'Sit down John Henry,' he said as Doc Holliday returned. 'I was just about to explain. My flight has been brought forward so I have to forgo pleasantries and get down to business. Firstly, Dr Ludgeworth, you have given my son Fabio a valuable lesson in standards and shown him that he needs to be a better judge of people, lessons that I am sure will be of great benefit to him. In recognition of your help my organisation has done two things, we cleared your problems following the incident at ...' he hesitated.

'Shrivellsea,' prompted Doc Holliday.

'Ah, yes, Shrivellsea, strange name, even for the English.' said Brindisi. 'I also, at John Henry's suggestion, looked into the matter of your American adventure. Any ban was never formalised and, should you so wish, you are free to return.' He leaned forward and smiled at Sludge. 'Do you have anything to say?'

Sludge looked about him, noticed two very large men, both dressed in similar fashion to Brindisi, standing to the left of the doorway. 'I don't know why you have done this.' he said slowly. 'Fabio will pass or fail by his own efforts. If you think that you can influence his results by doing favours for me then you are mistaken. However,' he glanced at Doc Holliday, who was showing signs of great concern, 'I am grateful for your assistance.'

The cold-eyed man stared at the Italian who held his gaze without any signs of emotion.

After an uncomfortable pause, Brindisi suddenly leaned forward and said briskly, 'No matter. Let's move on. Do you have the pubic hair with you?'

Startled and taken aback by the abruptness of the switch of topic and the directness of the question Sludge could only bluster, 'No, not with me.'

'Very sensible,' said Brindisi, ' I take it that you have left it with your London solicitor. What did you find out there?'

The cold-eyed man could feel the kid going under. He was out of his league. He looked at the big men standing near the doorway.

'I found some workbooks,' said Sludge, 'containing a great many new poems.'

'New poems?' said Brindisi, 'Are any about the Princess?'

'No, none at all,' said Sludge, 'funny that. There were poems about a great many people, including me, but none about her.'

'So, Dr Ludgeworth" Brindisi glanced at Doc Holliday and back at Sludge, 'if there were no poems, how do you know about the Princess?' He signalled one of the big men forward, motioned him to bend down and whispered in his ear. The big man nodded briefly, stared at Sludge for a few seconds, and left. 'And' Brindisi continued 'exactly what do you know about her?'

The cold-eyed man cursed. The kid had walked into that.

Sludge sighed and squirmed a little in his seat. He was very hot. He concentrated on the sensation made by a river of sweat that was running down the back of his neck. In his mind's eye, he saw a damp patch forming on his collar 'How very undignified.' he said to himself. Unaware that he had spoken out loud he was puzzled by the swift exchange of glances between Doc Holliday and Signor Brindisi. He noticed that there was only one big man standing near the doorway.

'Albert Bleaney kept a diary of sorts.' he said. 'Quite separate from the workbooks he left me an extract from the diary. The rest I assume he destroyed. The extract described how when he went to collect his OBE he was taken to a secluded garden where he met the Princess. He describes exactly how he came by the pubic hair. The diary extract and the pubic hair are in the safe keeping of my solicitor.'

'I assume that a man called Lombardo took him to the Princess.' said Brindisi.

'Yes,' Sludge said, 'but how do you know that?'

'Dr Ludgeworth,' said Brindisi, 'I know a great many things. Things you couldn't even dream about.' He glanced at his watch. 'Let me tell you a story. A story about a beautiful Princess, your Royal Family and matters of supposed national security.'

'Many years ago my grandfather, for reasons too complicated to explain here, met your King George and his Queen. As a result he became a fervent Royalist and a great admirer of your country. My father shared those passions and tried to pass them on to me. I spoke English from an early age and was encouraged to think of England as a second home. I do love England but think of your Royal Family as a dysfunctional unit, parasitical and self-absorbed. Does that surprise you?'

'No,' Sludge shrugged, 'that seems a reasonable view to me.' He was going to develop the theme, but a burdensome melancholy pressed on him, and after adding, 'I am not a lover of the Royal Family.' he remained silent.

Brindisi smiled and sipped his coffee. 'In 1988 I was fortunate enough to meet the Princess when she visited Italy with her fool of a husband. It was obvious that the marriage was not a good one. They had nothing in common. He was the dullest man, arrogant and drab, whereas she was fully alive, vital and invigorating.' His eyes became distant and his voice dropped almost to a whisper. 'She had the most incredible aura of an almost primitive sexuality combined with a sort of unknowing innocence, a naivety almost, that I found devastating. I fell in love with her.'

He picked up his coffee cup and saw that it was empty, after refilling his cup he offered the pot to Sludge who shook his head. Carefully Brindisi lifted the cup to his lips and took a small mouthful. 'We kept in regular touch until her death.' he said, 'I became a confidant, a father figure I believe.'

'Shortly after our first meeting I began to receive unverifiable reports about the Princess. For instance, one of the lies I was told that she was having an ongoing affair with the dictator of an unnamed African country. I was also told that she invented the 'chukka fucker' when one afternoon she serviced a whole polo team. I was able to discover that the widely circulated lies came out of your Whitehall, driven from the highest levels. Such attempts continued, even after her death she was pursued by those dogs.'

Brindisi's face darkened as he rubbed his hands together in a drying motion as if to rid himself of a stubborn stain. 'My investigations' he said, 'suggested very strongly that the rumours were untrue and part of a foul and clumsy plot to alienate and discredit her. The marriage was going wrong and she did not conform to the image the Royals had of themselves. So your English establishment was looking for ways to show that the popular Princess, the British Blossom as she was known to so many, was not as fragrant as had been supposed.'

Brindisi paused and looked around the room. 'Before I continue,' he said, 'I must make clear that I speak to you in absolute confidence. Nothing I say should be repeated, do I have your word on that?'

Sludge nodded his head with the briefest of movements and said in a flat emotionless voice, 'Go on with your story. I have classes to attend.'

Brindisi stared at Sludge before flicking his gaze at Doc Holliday who was looking intently at the floor between his feet. The Italian transferred his gaze to the doorway and saw that both the big men were standing there, he accepted without acknowledgement a hand signal from the man who had just returned to his post.

'One rumour,' he continued, 'could not be proved to be false, neither could it be substantiated. It was alleged that the Princess had given clippings of her pubic hair as mementoes to a privileged few, perhaps as many as six lucky recipients were involved. Although the story has been common knowledge in some quarters even your newspapers could not print such a scurrilous tale without evidence In spite of their diligent searching over the years the secret service, MI5, call them what you will, have not been able to produce such evidence, and so the story has remained an unsubstantiated rumour. Now, Dr Ludgeworth, by default almost, you have come into possession of not only the highly desired artefact itself, but also written evidence, establishing provenance as it were. The question is, Dr Ludgeworth, what are you going to do with your inheritance?'

The cold-eyed man grinned at the question. He opened a fresh pack of Marlboro and crumpled the cellophane before dropping it on the table. He watched it slowly unfolding as he lit his cigarette, then he lifted his eyes to meet the expressionless stare of the Italian. 'Inheritance?' he drawled, 'Sure is one hell of a gift.' By moving in his chair he could feel the warmth and comforting weight of his revolver pressing heavily on his hip. The cold-eyed man settled back and waited.

If he was at all taken aback by Sludge's response, Brindisi didn't show it. 'You have only two options.' he said. 'You cannot keep the goods. If you try to do that, they will be taken from you.' He shrugged, 'Perhaps even now your secret service is talking to Mr Cuthbert. Your options are to give away the goods, or, as they are extremely valuable, you could sell them. If they go to the secret service then they will assuredly find their way into the press, where they will cause a sensation, and the Princess will be branded a whore. On the other hand, if they come into my possession, they will vanish forever.'

'I should sound a note of caution.' said Brindisi, 'If you decide to go to the highest bidder you would do well to remember the fate of the man who tried to sell the bloodstained panties allegedly taken off the Princess following the fatal crash. The panties never materialised and the would be seller vanished.'

'No Billy!' shouted Doc Holliday in alarm as Sludge rose abruptly from his chair knocking against the table with enough force to dislodge the coffee pot onto the floor where it rolled into the path of the big men who began moving quickly towards Brindisi the moment Sludge stood up.

'The kid is no seller of panties.' snarled the cold-eyed man. 'He will decide what to do when he is good and ready.' He put his hand on the butt of his revolver and looked at the big men. 'Do you feel lucky?' he said. 'Everyone keep calm,' he ordered, 'me and the kid are going walk out of here, peaceable like.' The cold-eyed man backed slowly to the door, his gun hand hovering over his revolver. His eyes didn't leave the tableau of Brindisi, Doc Holliday and the big men until he reached the door, then after a swift glance over his shoulder, he turned and ran from the room.

Brindisi shook his head to prevent the big men from following Sludge and turned to Doc Holliday. 'Well, John Henry,' he said, 'can you tell me what that was all about?'

The Doc shook his head. 'He's ill, that much is obvious. I'll go and talk to him.' he said as he started to get to his feet.

'No,' Brindisi motioned to him to keep sitting, 'I want you to take Jimmy to talk to him. He will be here in about a couple of hours.' He stood up. 'Call me in Paris this evening. Jimmy will convince Ludgeworth of the wisdom of doing a deal with me - I look to you to close that deal. You can do whatever is necessary.' Brindisi straightened his tie and fastened his jacket. 'Do I make myself clear John Henry?' he said in a tone that discouraged discussion.

White-faced, Doc Holliday nodded, 'I'll see to that, Signor Brindisi.' he said unhappily.

In the Refectory - Some Soft Words, and then the Hard Word

'Apparently this Meredith chap, short bald man with a black goatee beard, volunteered his services during the Bleaney Walk. As he used to be a stock controller, Joan thought he was an ideal choice to help with the inventory at 105 West Bank. He did more than assist - he ran the show.'

Ann Gora laughed and looked for a response from Sludge, who merely nodded distractedly. She had arrived at the Refectory a little after two o'clock and thought that she had missed Sludge until she spotted him, sitting alone in an alcove, partly hidden behind an unlikely bank of imitation shrubs. Shaken by the difference in him since their meeting four days ago, she wondered whether his trance like state was due to delayed shock at the unfortunate death of Ronan Coyne or if other factors were involved.

'Anyway,' she went on, 'when I arrived at the house, just before nine o'clock, he had already taken photographs of every room, from every possible angle as far as I could determine. Joan introduced me to Beryl, Pamela and a lady, called Betty Turnbull I think, who wanted to begin with a minute's silence for Coyne that Joan dismissed out of hand. Meredith asked us to wait outside the house until he had finished. The photography completed, Meredith explained his 'strategic plan'.' She paused and watched as Sludge slowly poured salt onto the table, making a small pyramid.

'Strategic plan?' he muttered dully, as he worked a finger into the salt to make a small crater that he began to widen, changing the pyramid into a hollow circle.

'Yes,' said Ann with a brightness she did not feel, 'he explained that everything was to be listed and retained for future generations. All papers that had been written or typed on, including old envelopes, wrapping paper, address labels etcetera, he said was 'literature appertaining to the past'. Everything else, clothing, including socks and underwear, tables, chairs, light fittings, you name it, he said was of 'literary importance' because of their connection with the poet's house. He explained that such unlikely items as the dustbin were of possible literary significance as the diaries may have been burned in there.' She smiled at Sludge who methodically and with great concentration was attempting to transform the circle of salt into its previous pyramid shape.

'He insisted,' she continued, 'that all carpets were to be removed so that floorboards could be lifted and the under floor area examined. It wasn't until he suggested that the garden be dug over in case items of 'literary value' were buried there that Joan put her foot down. Are you interested in this, Billy?' she asked, not with impatience, but a frank puzzlement as Sludge's preoccupation with the salt grains appeared to render him completely unaware of her presence.

Sludge studied the result of his efforts carefully then holding the saltcellar several inches above the table allowed the contents to run onto the pile below. 'Let your speech be always with grace, seasoned with salt.' he said as he looked up briefly. 'Paul's letter to the Colossians.' he explained, 'Carry on.'

'OK,' she said, 'I'll give you the executive summary, Billy, more or less what I have said in my report. The house was searched very thoroughly, everything was listed and a copy of the inventory will go with my report. No evidence was found of any material that might be of interest to my employer. No evidence whatsoever. That is not to say that such never existed, but if it did it has been destroyed,' she paused momentarily, 'or removed.'

Taking a small pinch of salt between finger and thumb of his right hand Sludge dropped it over his left shoulder, 'It's an old superstition,' he said, 'the salt keeps the devil off your tail. Or something like that.' he shrugged.

Ann reached across the table and gripped Sludge's wrist. 'Listen to me Billy.' she said sharply, 'I need you to listen.' She shook his wrist, 'Are you listening?'

'You have my attention.' said Sludge mildly, his eyes on her, but focussed on an unknown point far away.

'I have also said that you cannot help us, that you know nothing.' She released Sludge's wrist and took hold of his hand. 'If I am shown to be wrong, Billy, if at some time it is seen that you were involved, I will be in serious trouble. At best my career would be over, but if I am thought to have been complicit, having no career would be the least of my troubles.' She squeezed his hand and leaned across the table. 'Is there anything you want to tell me?' she said very softly.

The cold-eyed man grinned to himself. Ann Gora was clever, but not clever enough. She had almost fooled the kid. The business in the park with the bicycle, the laughter, the friendliness, and now the handholding. It hadn't worked. The kid had seen through it all, he was strong.

'File your report.' he said.

Brushing the salt grains from her fingers, Ann Gora stared at Sludge for several seconds. 'I could help you, Billy,' she said, 'whatever it is you are going to do, I could help you.' She rested her hands on the table, palms upward, in a gesture of openness and vulnerability. 'You need help.' she said.

'Persistent bitch.' thought the cold-eyed man, 'File your report' he said.

Sludge stared at the back of her yellow sweater as Ann Gora walked away and then began an attempt to push the salt grains into a square. Busily occupied Sludge did not notice that two men stopped Ann Gora as she left the refectory.

'Excuse me,' said Doc Holliday, 'I believe you have seen Dr Ludgeworth. Is he still here?' Touching the brim of his hat in thanks as she pointed to the alcove, he wondered briefly at the tear-filled eyes, but when he turned to look back at her after glancing across at Sludge, she had gone.

As the two men advanced on the alcove Doc Holliday remained some distance away, allowing his companion to approach Sludge alone. Wearing a red blouson over a white tee shirt, blue denims and motorcycle boots, the man ran his fingers through his dark blond hair as he sat down opposite Sludge.

'Hello Dr Ludgeworth,' he said 'my name is James Dean.'

'Of course it is.' said Sludge dryly, raising an eyebrow.

'I understand that you have done a deal with my boss, Mr Brindisi.' the man said.

Sludge shook his head slowly. 'I've met Mr Brindisi' he said, 'we talked about his son. I don't know anything about a deal.'

'Sure you do, you have agreed to give something to Mr Brindisi in return for a sizeable consideration. You remember now?' Taking a comb from the back pocket of his jeans he ran it through his hair, patted the front into shape, blew across the teeth of the comb and slipped it back into his pocket. 'Sure you remember.' He grinned, showing perfectly regular white teeth.

'Mr Dean,' began Sludge

'Hey, call me Jimmy.' said the man.

Sludge sighed. Another game had started. 'Jimmy,' he said, rubbing his eyes, 'I don't know what you're talking about.'

Jimmy turned up the collar of his blouson and looked around him while unwrapping a stick of chewing gum. 'I work for Mr Brindisi,' he said, 'I'm his contracts manager. After a deal is set up I make certain that it is honoured and any conditions are followed exactly. One of the conditions of your deal, even if you decide to pull out, is that you never talk about it, so - so far, so good.'

'I still don't know what you are talking about.' Sludge said doggedly.

'OK, OK,' the man said, 'I've got the message.' He blew his chewing gum into a small bubble that popped and stuck to his upper lip. After scraping the gum back into his mouth with his bottom teeth he went on, 'Now, I have a message for you from the Board. It is about consequences.' He glanced around him. 'Break the deal and you die.' he said with a matter of fact nonchalance. 'It's as simple as that. You die, and anyone you have told dies too.' He popped another small bubble and stared at Sludge, his face suddenly hard and impassive.

Sludge felt his throat constrict and his breathing became difficult. Looking over the man's head, he could see Doc Holliday watching them, extreme anxiety in his face. 'The Doc didn't think this was necessary,' the man said, 'he said you are a man of honour. The others thought honour or not, you need to know about consequences.' The man glanced over his shoulder in the direction of Doc Holliday, looking back at Sludge he said, 'He particularly didn't want you to be given proof. The others didn't agree. They said 'He's a school teacher he might think consequences mean getting his legs slapped, or being told 'naughty boy, don't do it again'. Give him proof.' they said.'

He reached inside his blouson and took out a paper bag from which he extracted a small replica coffin, about five inches long, that he placed in front of Sludge. He folded the bag, put it in his pocket, and then placed a cupped hand either side of the coffin. 'Open it.' he said.

Sludge stared at the small black object lying between the man's long, slender, surprisingly delicate hands and noted the detail, tiny silver handles, silver hinges, and a silver cross on the lid. He became aware of a fierce ringing inside his head and loosened his collar as his face began to burn. The coffin and the man's hands seemed to waver to and fro as he stared down at them.

The man leaned across the table, his menacing air overwhelming, yet casual in a way that made it more palpable. 'Open it.' he said, pushing the coffin closer with his thumbs.

Sludge's hand trembled as he reached out. The box was surprisingly cold and the lid opened easily, releasing a vaguely unpleasant odour. He had to blink several times to focus his eyes. The coffin was lined in red silk and contained a finger. The fingernail was bitten down and the other end bloodied. He wondered afterwards why he noticed those details first before he saw the ring. Just below the knuckle was a large silver ring with a black stone on which the initials, PEP, were engraved in silver. Sludge stared at the ring in bemusement for a few seconds before he realised that he was looking at a finger that had once belonged to Peter Edgar Pelham.

He had just enough time to turn his head away from the table before he was violently sick. The pain in his head overwhelmed him and with a low moan Sludge slid from his chair and collapsed into the pool of vomit where he lay absolutely motionless.

FIFTEEN

In the fading light of a December afternoon, against the dark backcloth of the mountains, Billy Sludge watched the first snows of winter drift out of a windless sky. He breathed deeply, sucking the clean, cold air to the very bottom of his lungs and smiled as he cycled along Main Street, heading towards the Western Hat and Boot Emporium - Hand Made A Speciality.

He had been in Durango, Colorado, for six weeks. For the first couple of weeks he had stayed at the Rochester Hotel on East Second Street a place that described itself as a 'funky cowboy' hotel. Then he had moved into a three-roomed apartment over Maxine's bookshop and record store where he planned to stay for a while. Maxine also drove the Airport taxi and collected Sludge from La Plata airport just outside of town when he arrived from London Heathrow, via Chicago and Denver.

At the suggestion of Fran Cuthbert, the Chicago to Denver leg of his trip was by Amtrak train. On the train he was in the company of a group of the Amish, who were friendly in a self-contained way, had dinner with an elderly Sinophobe, and met a young woman on her way to San Francisco who expressed distaste at his Durango destination, calling it a place of 'cowboys and bikers', only for her to be discomfited by Sludge's wide grin and cheery response of, 'Sounds like my kind of place.'

If Charles Cuthbert knew the identity of the woman who telephoned him one Thursday night in May with the news that Sludge was very ill and might also be in serious trouble, he never revealed that identity. Early the next day he had collected Sludge from Kingston and taken him to Fuller's Priory, a retreat in remote countryside, some miles south of Oxford. Fran Cuthbert often used the Priory, which was run by a long-term trusted associate, when her patients needed a period of undisturbed rest. Sludge was there for almost a month before, by mutual consent, he moved to stay with the Cuthberts in North London, where he talked, and Fran Cuthbert listened.

In the meantime, Charles Cuthbert took on the role of adviser and friend. He negotiated that Sludge could take a one year sabbatical leave from the University and, after a short but detailed discussion about the disappearance of Dr Peter Pelham, reached an agreement with Signor Paolo Brindisi that Sludge would make a decision on the disposal of 'the goods' in no more than twelve months time. Brindisi agreed to wait on the condition that either the goods were passed to him, perhaps for a consideration or a donation to charity, or they were destroyed in front of his eyes. This condition was accepted.

Shortly afterwards, Sludge asked Charles to act as his literary agent. In addition to accepting this role, Charles also gave guarded reports on his health and progress to an unnamed woman who telephoned on a weekly basis. He also passed on an address and invitation to visit from Doc Holliday together with the news that he had settled 'more or less permanently' in Barcelona.

In order that Sludge could travel relatively unencumbered with baggage, Charles made arrangements to ship separately, clothes, books and other personal items. To his credit, he did not so much as even raise an eyebrow when Sludge asked for his bicycle to be added to the list. The cargo had been delivered to La Plata a few days a⸴ to be collected by Maxine and already Sludge becoming a familiar sight as he cycled around th his long jacket open and billowing behind him.

219

Even though dusk was approaching, and it was snowing, the portly, middle aged, bearded man on the Harley Davidson motorcycle was wearing sunglasses as he coasted slowly down the near deserted street. 'Yo, Billy.' he called, pulling alongside the gently cruising Sludge, 'How's the writing going?'

'Writing's going fine.' said Sludge, glancing across at the motorcyclist. 'Just fine.'

The man nodded, 'I'll be in Strater's Bar later, catch you then, Billy.' he said, as he pulled into the centre of the road and continued his leisurely progress through town. Sludge watched the taillight of the Harley recede and wondered if that was Fat Fred McDobson, or his brother, Fat Frank. Even under the lights of Strater's Bar he couldn't tell them apart.

The town of Durango was in two distinct parts, some two miles apart. The modern mountain resort was where the majority of the fourteen thousand inhabitants lived and worked and the older part, known as Animas City when it was founded back in 1860, was located at the head of the Durango to Silverton Railroad on the Animas River. When Sludge learned that 18th Century Spanish explorers named the river, Rio De Las Animas Perdidas - the River of Lost Souls - he allowed himself a wry smile. He had settled into the old part of town and had been readily accepted by the few hundred or so people who lived there and who knew him as a writer, who was 'writing not one book, but two. One's about a dead English poet and the other is about some Western stories left by his pa'. Maxine gleaned this information from Sludge as she drove him from the Airport and it was very soon passed around town.

The hat shop still had a tethering rail outside for the benefit of its horse borne customers. Whether it was authentic or not Sludge did not know, but smiled to himself as he secured his bicycle to the wooden pole, barely resisting the strong temptation to slap the saddle while saying, 'steady old fellow'.

'Do you think it is worth stealing?'

Sludge glanced up at the softly mocking enquiry and saw that the hat shop owner, Joel Ford, was watching from the open front door.

'Probably not', laughed Sludge, 'but it would be like losing an old friend.' he said as he crossed the sidewalk to take Joel's outstretched hand.

'What do you think?' said Joel anxiously, as Sludge regarded himself in the mirror. 'Is it what you wanted?'

Sludge turned his head this way and that to examine the effect of his new hat from different angles. He tipped the hat, a hard top bowler with a curled brim, (an almost exact replica of that worn by Paul Newman in *Butch Cassidy and The Sundance Kid*) drawled, 'the fall will probably kill you,' and laughed.

'Joel,' he said, 'this is absolutely fine. Thanks for your trouble.'

'My pleasure, Billy.' said Joel, his tanned face creased with delight, not only because Sludge was satisfied, but also he had recognised the quotation from the film and furthermore, Sludge's attempt at a western drawl, although enthusiastic, was quite the worst he had ever heard.

A few days later, standing in the middle of the car park at La Plata Airport, Ann Fielden - she had abandoned the Gora pseudonym when she resigned from the department and ceremonially burned the yellow sweater - shivered slightly, and drew her coat more tightly around her. She was beginning to feel a little foolish. The woman (Maxine? - Ann hadn't quite caught her name) who had met her off the airplane had walked her to the car park and asked her to wait there while she attended to some business. That was several minutes ago, and there was no sign of her. She shivered again and was about to go back into the Airport lounge when she heard someone singing. Puzzled, she looked towards the far end of the low single story building as the singing, which was getting louder, came from that direction.

To her astonishment, a cyclist burst around the corner singing, 'raindrops keep falling on my head, la la la la la la la la la la. '

'Billy Sludge, what are you doing!' Ann clapped her hands delightedly and joined in the song as the singing Sludge rode a wide circle around her.

He stopped in front of her. 'Hello, Ann.' he said, 'It's been a time. Good to see you again.'

'Hello, Billy,' she said, 'It's so good to see you. Love the hat - and the bike, it's surely not the same one? The one we rode in the park?'
'Yes' it is.' said Billy. 'Didn't I ever tell you?' he took her arm and wheeling his bicycle they walked towards

Maxine's pick-up. 'Didn't I ever tell you?' he repeated, so gravely that Ann glanced quickly at him

'This,' he said, 'was Mr Bleaney's bike.' Then he laughed.

SIXTEEN

The cold-eyed man rode north at a steady canter through the wooded slopes of the Rockies. He stopped once to look back in the direction of a small town he had left some time ago, but it was out of sight. As dusk closed in, he could see lights appearing here and there in the valley far below.

Night had fallen before he reached a long and narrow clearing leading to a fast running creek. Although he could smell snow in the air the sky was clear and the moon was casting shadows all around. He dismounted and walked his horse to the water. He lit a Marlboro and blew a thin stream of blue smoke into the crisp night air. As he did so a voice called out from the edge of the clearing.

'That you, Durango?

The cold-eyed man turned and grinned. 'Hello Tex,' he said as a short stocky man with a grizzled beard stepped forward, 'it's been a long time.'

'Too long, Durango,' said Tex as he embraced the cold-eyed man, 'too long.'

Both men stood in silence before Tex spoke again. 'How's my boy?' he said, his voice quiet and controlled. 'How's Young Billy?'

The cold-eyed man drew on his cigarette and looked up at the cloudless sky. 'I couldn't tèll you anything other than he's had a bad time, Tex. A very bad time. I had to step in for a while, or he wouldn't have made it through. I reckon he's gonna be OK now, leastways, he doesn't need me anymore.'

Tex nodded, 'I'm grateful, Durango.' he said, adding after a short pause, 'Are you going anywhere special?'

'Nowhere special. Just riding.'

'Mind if I tag along?'

'That'll be fine, Tex', said the Durango Kid, 'mighty fine.'

The two friends mounted their horses and rode across the creek, heading into the trees as a light snow began to fall.